The Good Neighbors

the Good Neighbors

BY

HOLLY BLACK
& TED NAIFEH

book one
KIN

New York   Toronto   London   Auckland   Sydney   Mexico City   New Delhi   Hong Kong   Buenos Aires

Text copyright © 2008 by Holly Black
Art copyright © 2008 by Ted Naifeh

This book was originally published in hardcover by Graphix in 2008.

ISBN-13: 978-0-439-85565-5
ISBN-10: 0-439-85565-9

10 9 8 7 6 5 4 3 2 1   09 10 11 12 13 14/0

First Scholastic paperback printing, October 2009
"Good Neighbors" title lettering by Jessica Hische
Lettering by John Green
Edited by David Levithan
Book design by Phil Falco
Creative Director: David Saylor
Printed in the U.S.A.   23

WEST CITY, THURSDAY EVENING.

MY NAME IS RUE, LIKE *KANGAROO* OR LIKE "YOU'LL *RUE* THE DAY WE MET, MWA-HA-HA!"

TUMS

I DON'T SWEAT STUFF. WORRYING JUST GIVES YOU WRINKLE LINES OR STRESS HIVES OR AN ACID STOMACH YOU CAN'T SOOTHE WITH A WHOLE BOX OF TUMS.

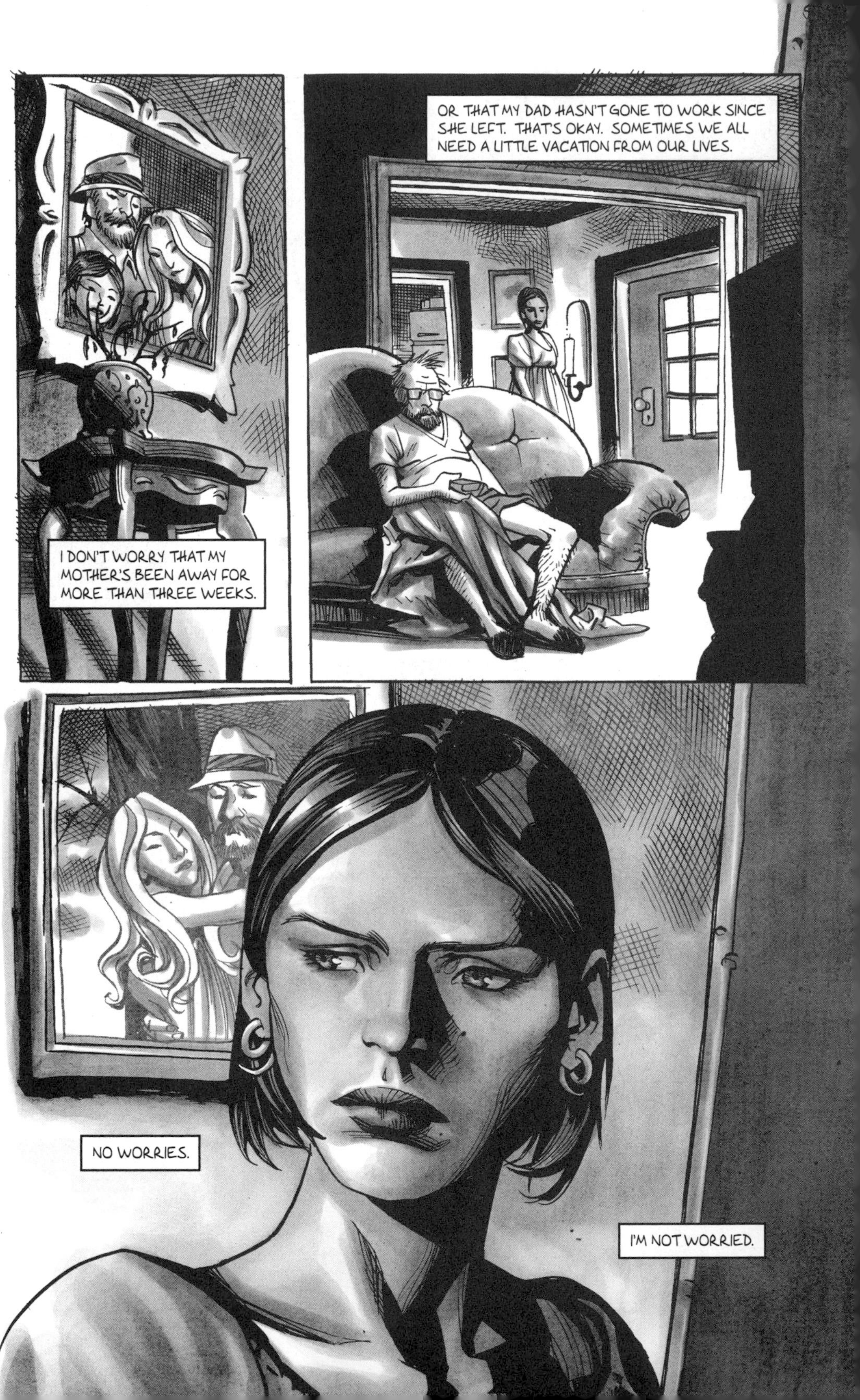
I DON'T WORRY THAT MY MOTHER'S BEEN AWAY FOR MORE THAN THREE WEEKS.
OR THAT MY DAD HASN'T GONE TO WORK SINCE SHE LEFT. THAT'S OKAY. SOMETIMES WE ALL NEED A LITTLE VACATION FROM OUR LIVES.
NO WORRIES.
I'M NOT WORRIED.

HONK!

YOU WANT ME TO BRING YOU BACK ANYTHING?

RIGHT. OKAY. BYE, DAD.

COME ON, RUE-TERINO. IN YOU GET. PLACES TO DO AND THINGS TO GO.

HOW ARE YOU DOING? ANY WORD FROM YOUR MA?

NOTHING. BUT IT'S COOL. SHE'LL TURN UP SOON. WHERE ELSE HAS SHE GOT TO GO?

I'VE GOT *JUST* THE TROUBLE TO GET YOUR MIND OFF OF THINGS.

HOW ABOUT YOU LEAN UP HERE AND GIVE ME A *BIG WET ONE?* I HAVE BEEN TOLD MY TONGUE IS *VERY* RELAXING.

YOU ARE SUCH A *DIRTBAG,* JUSTIN.

YOU KNOW HOW SOMETIMES, WHEN YOU GLANCE AT SOMETHING OUT OF THE CORNER OF YOUR EYE, IT LOOKS DIFFERENT FOR A MOMENT?

EARTH TO RUE. WHAT ARE YOU LOOKING AT?

WELL, SOMETIMES WHEN I LOOK STRAIGHT AT A THING, IT LOOKS WEIRD, TOO. AND THOSE MOMENTS ARE STRETCHING WIDER AND WIDER.

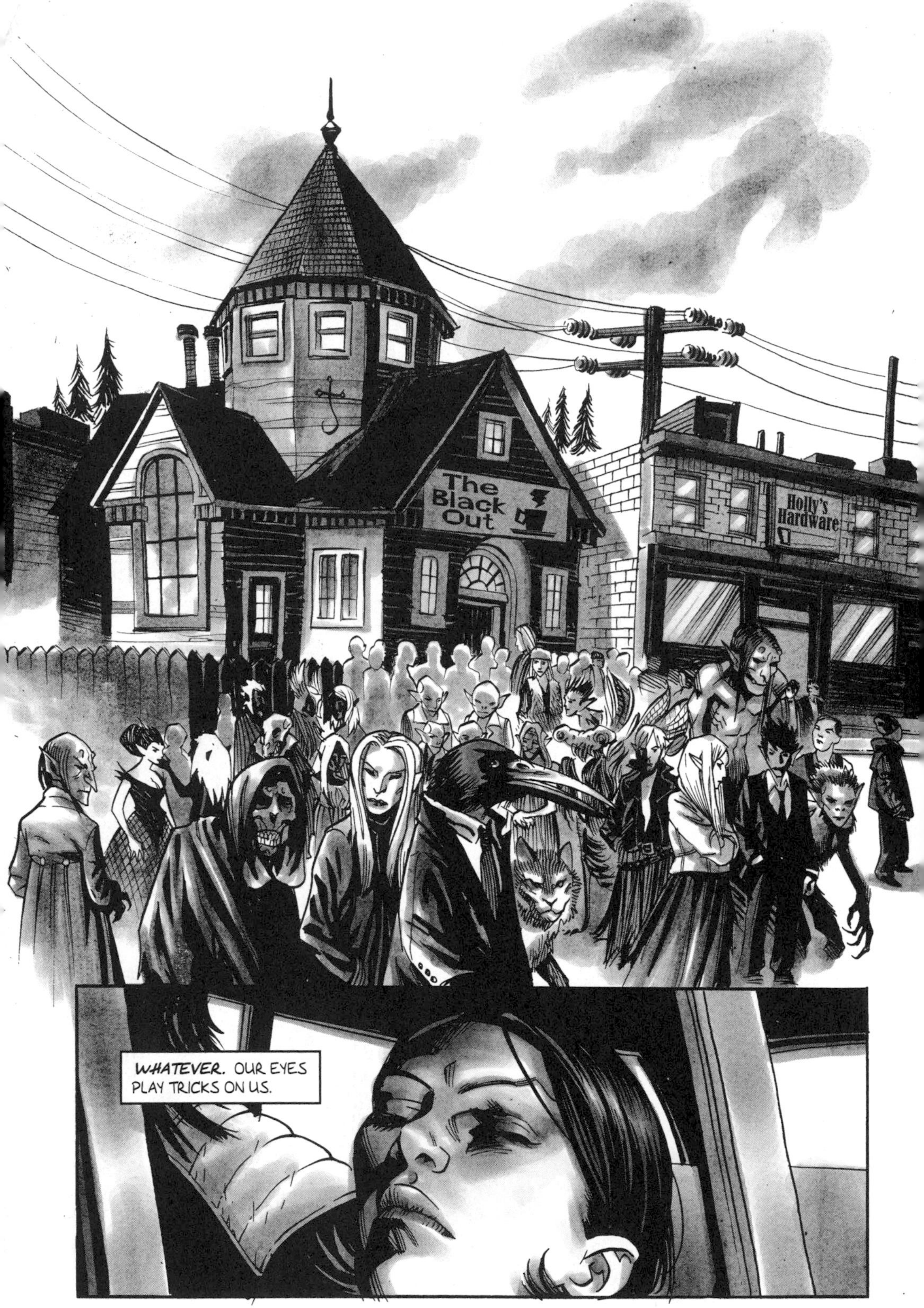
The Black Out
Holly's Hardware
WHATEVER. OUR EYES PLAY TRICKS ON US.

I NEED A QUADRUPLE SHOT. I WANT MY BLOOD TO RUN BLACK WITH JAVA.

I SAW YOUR SHOW ON FRIDAY. YOU *ROCKED*.

THEY'RE PLAYING AGAIN NEXT SUNDAY AT THE FLOODLIGHT.

RUE!

WHAT? YOU WANT TO BE MR. *COOL ALOOF ROCK GOD*?

PRETTY MUCH. AND YOU'RE RUINING IT.

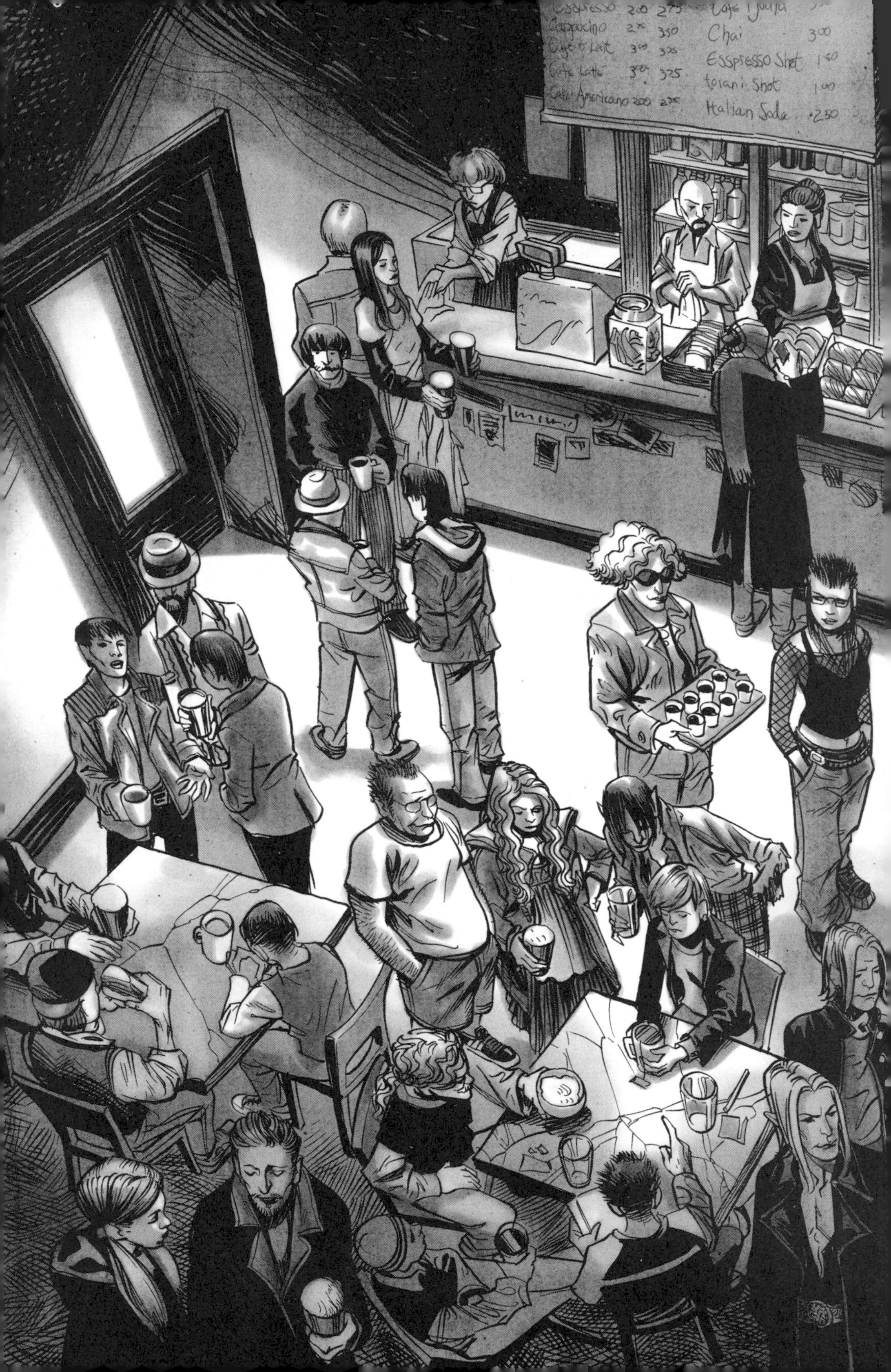
Cappucino 350
Cafe Latte 325
Cafe Americano 200
Chai 300
Esspresso Shot 150
torani Shot 100
Italian Soda 250

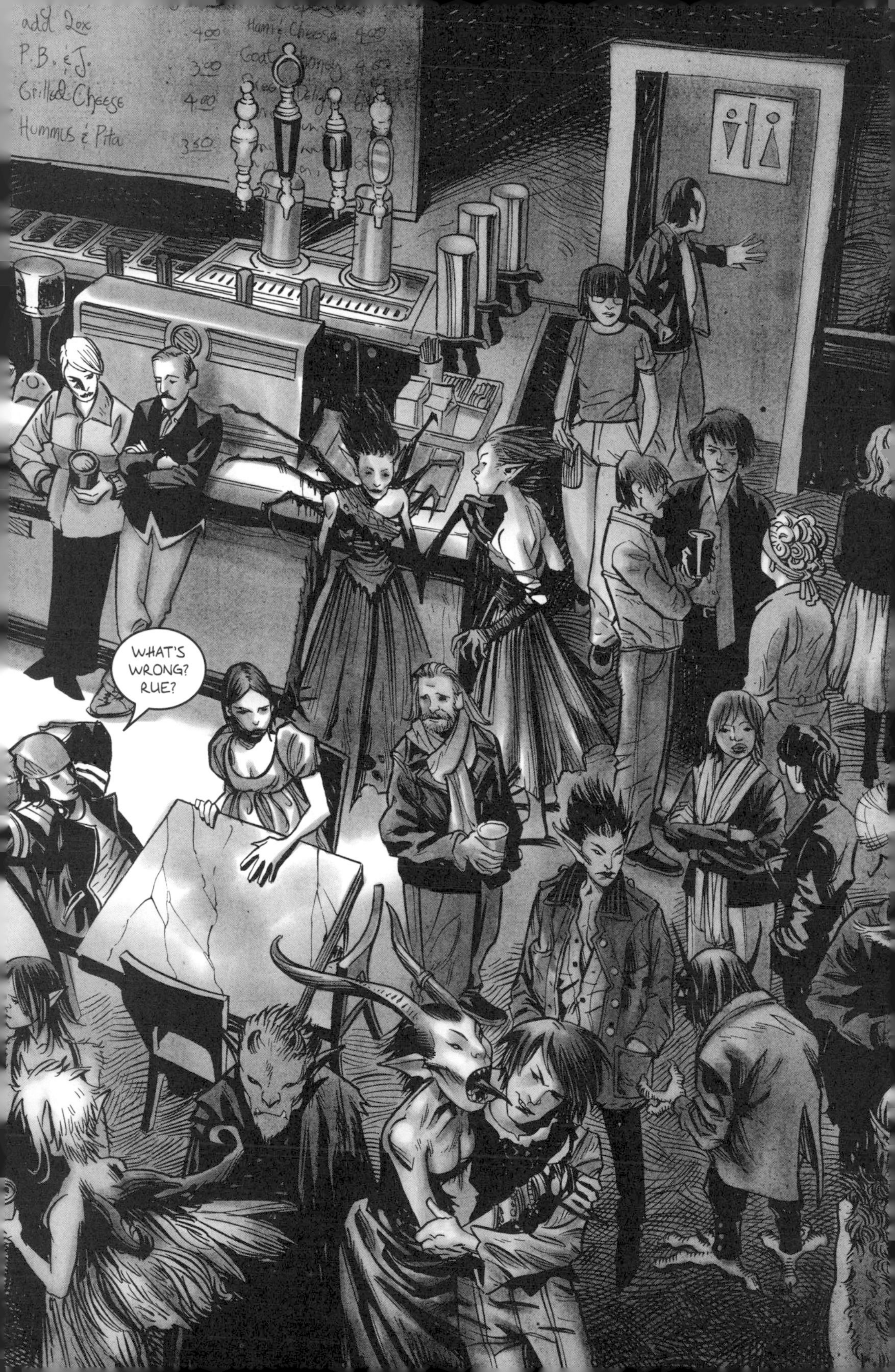
add Lox 4.00
P.B. & J. 3.00
Grilled Cheese 4.00
Hummus & Pita 3.50
Ham & Cheese 4.00
WHAT'S WRONG? RUE?

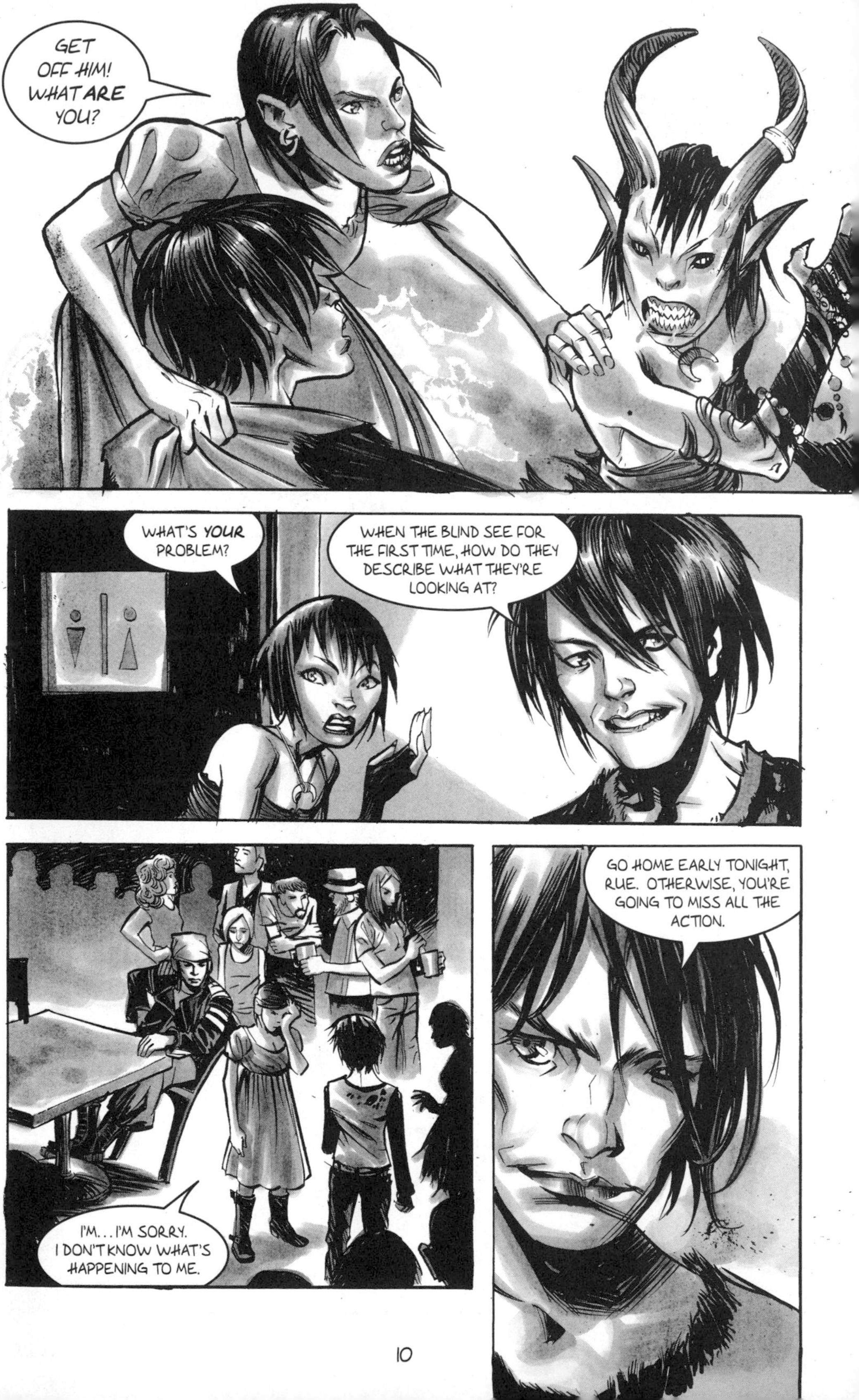
GET OFF HIM! WHAT ARE YOU?
WHAT'S YOUR PROBLEM?
WHEN THE BLIND SEE FOR THE FIRST TIME, HOW DO THEY DESCRIBE WHAT THEY'RE LOOKING AT?
I'M. . . I'M SORRY. I DON'T KNOW WHAT'S HAPPENING TO ME.
GO HOME EARLY TONIGHT, RUE. OTHERWISE, YOU'RE GOING TO MISS ALL THE ACTION.

READY TO DO SOME SHOTS?

WHAT WAS THAT? DO YOU KNOW THAT GUY?

I'VE NEVER SEEN HIM BEFORE.

THEN HOW DID HE KNOW YOUR NAME?

I DON'T KNOW!

I NEED TO GET SOME AIR.

I HEARD THEM ARGUING THE NIGHT SHE DISAPPEARED.

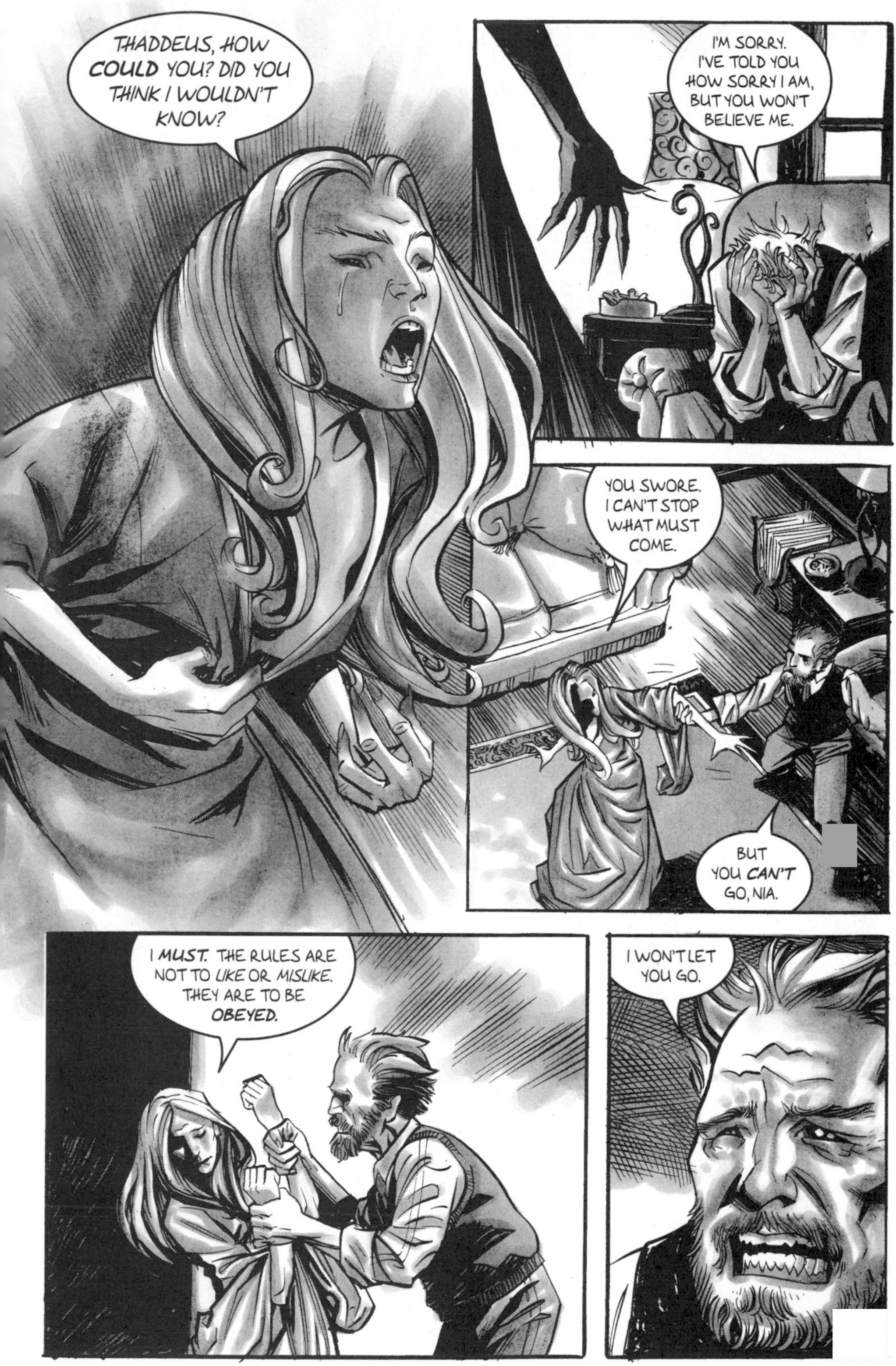
THADDEUS, HOW **COULD** YOU? DID YOU THINK I WOULDN'T KNOW?
I'M SORRY. I'VE TOLD YOU HOW SORRY I AM, BUT YOU WON'T BELIEVE ME.
YOU SWORE. I CAN'T STOP WHAT MUST COME.
BUT YOU **CAN'T** GO, NIA.
I **MUST.** THE RULES ARE NOT TO *LIKE* OR *MISLIKE.* THEY ARE TO BE **OBEYED.**
I WON'T LET YOU GO.

WHEN YOU TOUCHED HER, I WAS ALREADY GONE.

DO YOU KNOW WHAT IT'S LIKE TO BE WITH SOMEONE WHO DOESN'T KNOW EVEN THE *SMALLEST THING* ABOUT BEING HUMAN?

I CAN'T BE ANYTHING OTHER THAN WHAT I AM.

YOU HAVE TO STAY. I CAN'T BEAR IT IF YOU GO. I *WON'T* BEAR IT. I SWEAR, I'LL STOP YOU.

AAAAAAHH!!

THUD

MOM?

SHE HAD TO GO AWAY FOR A WHILE.

15

ARE YOU IN THERE, RUE? ARE YOU FEELING OKAY?

NOTHING TO WORRY ABOUT. NO WORRIES.

WASSAMATTER?

I'M BETTER. JUST GOT A LITTLE LIGHTHEADED.

I KEPT EXPECTING MY MOTHER TO COME BACK. I KEPT LOOKING FOR HER.

THAT WAS WHEN I STARTED TO SEE THINGS.

YOU SURE YOU'RE OKAY?

I'M *FINE*.

COULDN'T HAVE SAID IT BETTER. YOU'RE SO FINE YOU BLOW MY MIND.

JUSTIN, LUCY, DALE, AND I KIND OF HAVE THIS WEEKEND TRADITION.

WE GET COFFEE.

WE PICK AN ABANDONED BUILDING. ONE WITH SOME HISTORY.

WE BREAK IN.

WE TAKE PICTURES.

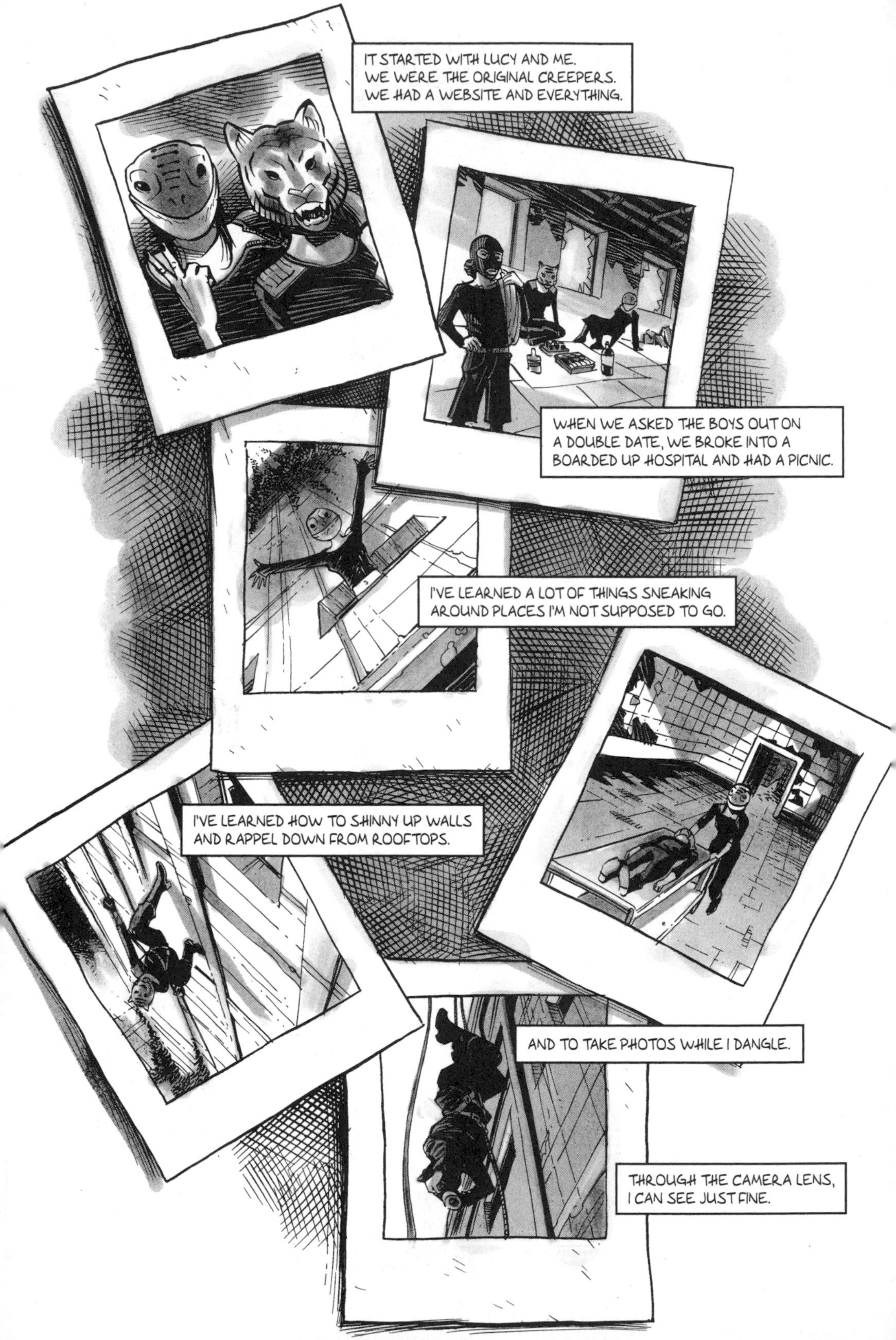
IT STARTED WITH LUCY AND ME. WE WERE THE ORIGINAL CREEPERS. WE HAD A WEBSITE AND EVERYTHING.
WHEN WE ASKED THE BOYS OUT ON A DOUBLE DATE, WE BROKE INTO A BOARDED UP HOSPITAL AND HAD A PICNIC.
I'VE LEARNED A LOT OF THINGS SNEAKING AROUND PLACES I'M NOT SUPPOSED TO GO.
I'VE LEARNED HOW TO SHINNY UP WALLS AND RAPPEL DOWN FROM ROOFTOPS.
AND TO TAKE PHOTOS WHILE I DANGLE.
THROUGH THE CAMERA LENS, I CAN SEE JUST FINE.

IT'S WEIRD ABOUT ALL THESE VINES. LATELY ALL THE OLD BUILDINGS HAVE THEM.

LIKE KUDZU OR SOMETHING.

LET ME TAKE A PICTURE OF THIS.

HEY!

THE VIEW'S AMAZING. GET UP HERE.

YOU CAN SEE FOR MILES AND MILES.

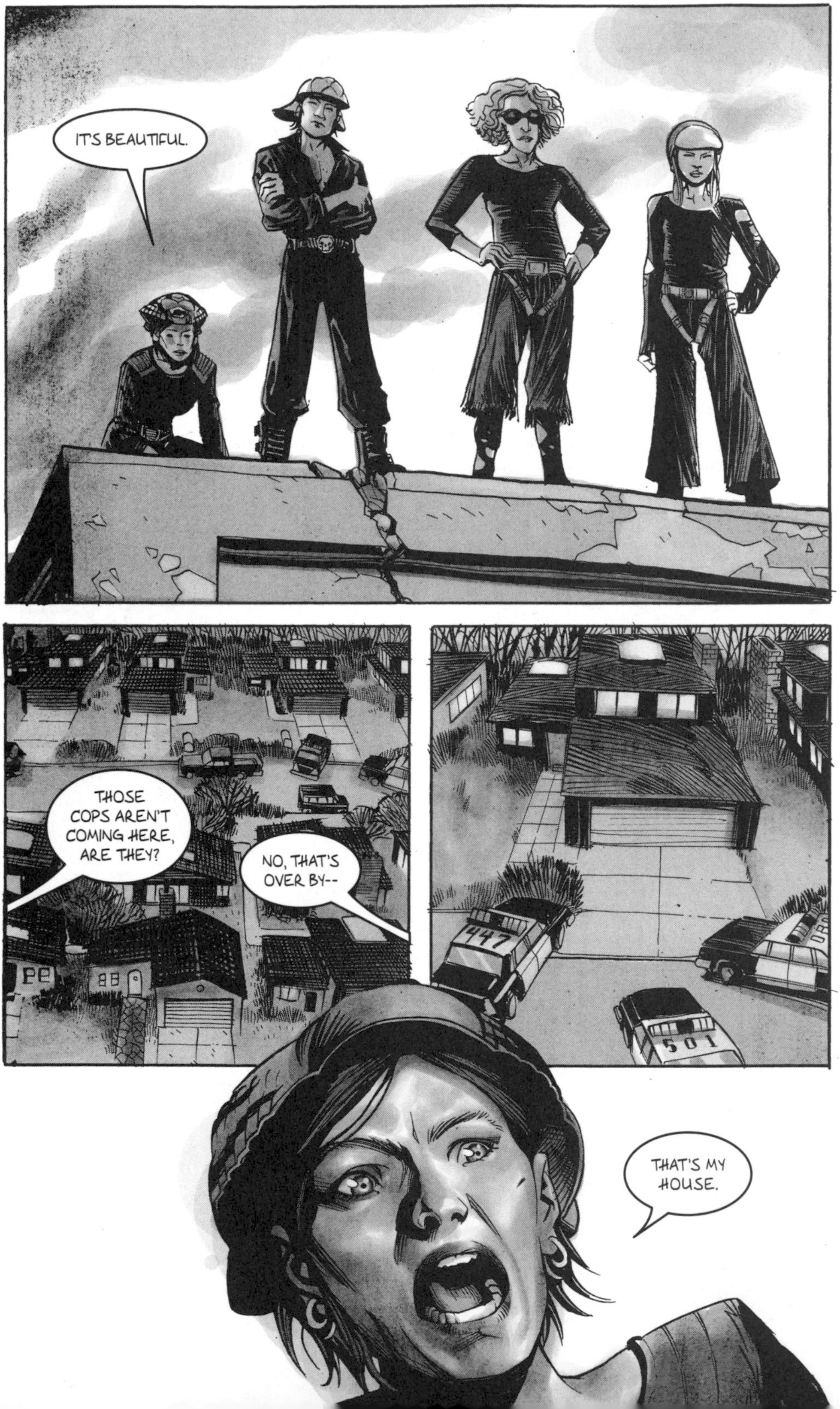
IT'S BEAUTIFUL.
THOSE COPS AREN'T COMING HERE, ARE THEY?
NO, THAT'S OVER BY--
447
501
THAT'S MY HOUSE.

I DIDN'T EVEN KNOW SARASA NARAYAN WAS DEAD!

THAT'S MY DAD! WHAT ARE YOU DOING?

WHY DON'T YOU COME WITH US TO THE STATION AND WE CAN EXPLAIN EVERYTHING?

YOUR NEIGHBOR SAID YOUR MOTHER'S BEEN MISSING FOR SEVERAL WEEKS.

YES, BUT WHAT DOES THAT HAVE TO DO WITH - ?

NO WORRIES.

I'M NOT WORRIED.

After I explained how long my mom had been gone, you could tell what they were thinking.

I came as soon as I heard.

The arresting officer says there's really nothing we can do until the morning.

What did Dad do?

AMANDA VALIA IS A HISTORY PROFESSOR AT BENTON COLLEGE, WHERE MY DAD TEACHES. THEY MET IN GRAD SCHOOL.

YOUR DAD DIDN'T DO ANYTHING.

IF IT WASN'T FOR HER, I'M PRETTY SURE DAD WOULD'VE BEEN FIRED BY NOW. SHE'S BEEN COVERING HIS CLASSES AND KEEPING US FED.

THANKS.

IT'S A WONDER SHE'S NOT SICK OF US.

I CONVINCED THEM YOU'D BE OKAY WITH ME FOR TONIGHT, BUT WE HAVE TO COME BACK AFTER SCHOOL TOMORROW.

NOTICE

IF ANYONE ASKS, I'M YOUR AUNT.

HOPEFULLY THIS WHOLE THING WILL BE STRAIGHTENED OUT BY THEN.

WHO'S SARASA NARAYAN?

SHE WAS ONE OF YOUR DAD'S STUDENTS. THEY JUST FOUND... THEY FOUND HER BODY. BUT IT HAS NOTHING TO DO WITH YOUR FATHER.

I KNOW THIS IS HARD ON YOU.

YOUR DAD NEEDS YOU TO BE BRAVE FOR HIM.

THIS WILL ALL BE OVER SOON.

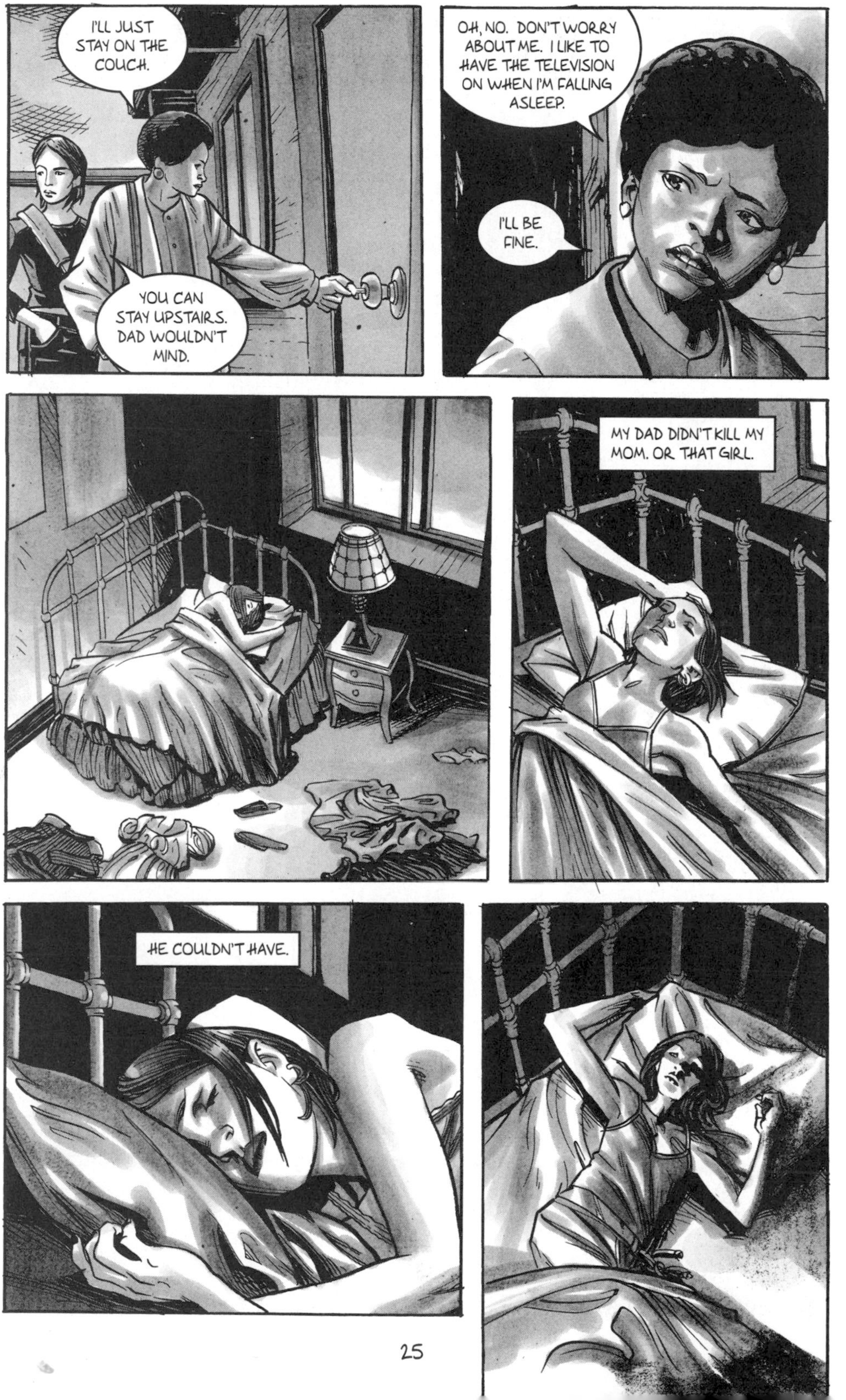
I'LL JUST STAY ON THE COUCH.
YOU CAN STAY UPSTAIRS. DAD WOULDN'T MIND.
OH, NO. DON'T WORRY ABOUT ME. I LIKE TO HAVE THE TELEVISION ON WHEN I'M FALLING ASLEEP.
I'LL BE FINE.
MY DAD DIDN'T KILL MY MOM. OR THAT GIRL.
HE COULDN'T HAVE.

WHY DIDN'T DAD LOOK FOR HER?

WHERE COULD MOM HAVE GONE?

WHAT DID SHE LEAVE BEHIND?

BIRTH CERTIFICATES FOR ME AND MY FATHER, BUT NONE FOR MY MOTHER. NO SOCIAL SECURITY CARD.

WEDDING, BUT NO MARRIAGE LICENSE. NO PICTURES OF MOM AS A KID. SHE LOOKS LIKE SHE'S NEVER AGED.

STRANGE.

THE BOY AT THE BLACKOUT. BUT THIS PICTURE IS FROM ALMOST TWENTY YEARS AGO.

...

FROM: DALE
R U OK?
SLEEP TIGHT.

WHERE DID YOU COME FROM, MOM?

AND WHERE DID YOU GO?

FRIDAY MORNING.

TODAY, AT SCHOOL, EVERYTHING IS DIFFERENT. THE COLORS SEEM BRIGHTER.

AND, OF COURSE, I'M CRAZY. THAT'S DIFFERENT, TOO.

WHAT HAPPENED?

SORRY I FREAKED OUT LAST NIGHT.

YOU DON'T HAVE TO APOLOGIZE FOR ANYTHING.

WHAT ARE YOU EVEN DOING AT SCHOOL?

I HEARD THEY'RE ACCUSING YOUR DAD OF KILLING A STUDENT.

WHAT, DID SHE NEVER DO THE READING?

IT'S A MISTAKE. SOMEONE MADE A MISTAKE.

SHE WAS ON THE NEWS.

SARASA WAS AN ENGLISH MAJOR, THE REPORTER SAID.

ACCORDING TO HER BROTHER, SHE STAYED BEHIND TO SPEAK WITH A PROFESSOR.

HER ROOMMATE REPORTED HER MISSING THREE DAYS LATER.

A FRESHMAN FOUND HER BODY.

THEY SAY THAT STRANGULATION IS A PRETTY PERSONAL CRIME. I GUESS BECAUSE YOU HAVE TO BE SO CLOSE.

JUSTIN!

I DIDN'T MEAN ANYTHING BY IT! ALL MURDERS ARE MORE LIKELY TO BE COMMITTED BY SOMEONE THE MURDERED PERSON KNOWS.

I'VE GOT TO GO.

RUE, I'M SORRY –

WHAT'S THE MATTER? DO YOU NEED HELP WITH YOUR HYPOTHESIS?

I NEED A PASS. RIGHT NOW.

RIGHT NOW.

WHAT ARE YOU?

I'M BORED, THAT'S WHAT I AM. BUT THE WORD YOU ARE LOOKING FOR IS FAERIE.

FAERIE? LIKE THE TOOTH FAIRY?

I DON'T CARE ABOUT TEETH. HOW COME YOU CAN SEE ME? AREN'T YOU A MORTAL GIRL?

AM I NOT SUPPOSED TO?

MOST PEOPLE CAN'T. UNLESS I LET THEM.

AND I'M NOT LETTING YOU.

I'VE BEEN SEEING A LOT OF THINGS LATELY.

CHOMP

THINGS YOU SHOULDN'T? THINGS LIKE ME?

WHAT DOES THAT MEAN?

MAYBE YOU'RE NOT A MORTAL GIRL, AFTER ALL. MAYBE YOU HAVE FAERIE BLOOD.

YOU'RE NOT A SELKIE OR SWANMAID ARE YOU? DID SOMEONE STEAL YOUR SKIN? DO WE NEED TO FIND IT AND FREE YOU?

NO! I DON'T EVEN KNOW WHAT THAT MEANS.

SOMETIMES WE STEAL AWAY HUMAN BABIES AND LEAVE FAERIES IN THEIR PLACE. CHANGELINGS. MAYBE YOU'RE ONE OF THOSE.

YOU STEAL... PEOPLE? BABIES? WHAT ABOUT ADULTS?

WHO ARE YOU TALKING TO?

34

YOU OKAY?

I'M SORRY ABOUT JUSTIN BEING SUCH A JERK. HE DOESN'T THINK.

THAT'S OKAY. I'M FINE. I'LL BE BACK IN CLASS IN A MINUTE.

IF YOU'RE SURE YOU'RE ALL RIGHT?

SURE, I'M SURE.

WAIT!

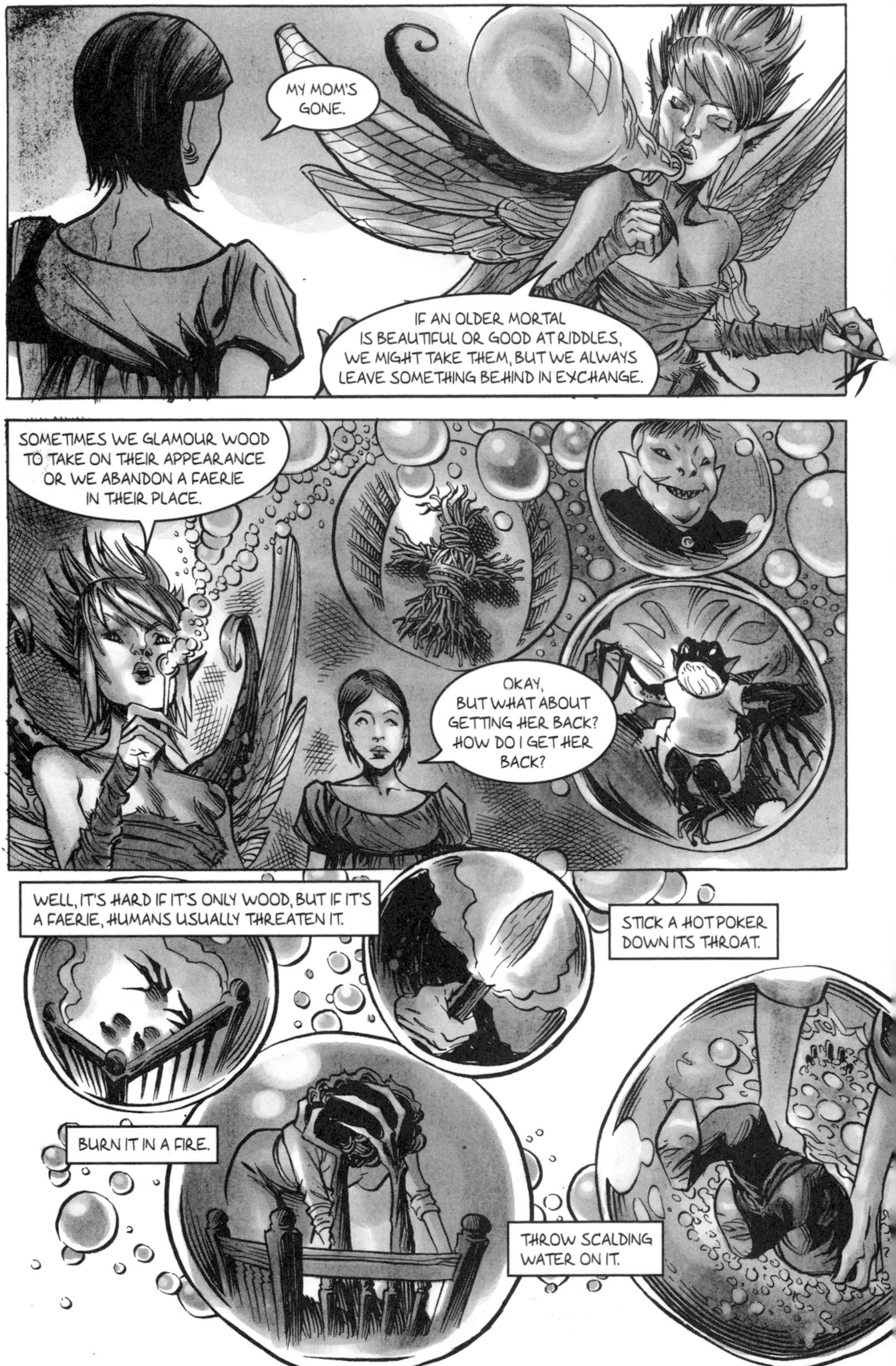
MY MOM'S GONE.
IF AN OLDER MORTAL IS BEAUTIFUL OR GOOD AT RIDDLES, WE MIGHT TAKE THEM, BUT WE ALWAYS LEAVE SOMETHING BEHIND IN EXCHANGE.
SOMETIMES WE GLAMOUR WOOD TO TAKE ON THEIR APPEARANCE OR WE ABANDON A FAERIE IN THEIR PLACE.
OKAY, BUT WHAT ABOUT GETTING HER BACK? HOW DO I GET HER BACK?
WELL, IT'S HARD IF IT'S ONLY WOOD, BUT IF IT'S A FAERIE, HUMANS USUALLY THREATEN IT.
STICK A HOT POKER DOWN ITS THROAT.
BURN IT IN A FIRE.
THROW SCALDING WATER ON IT.

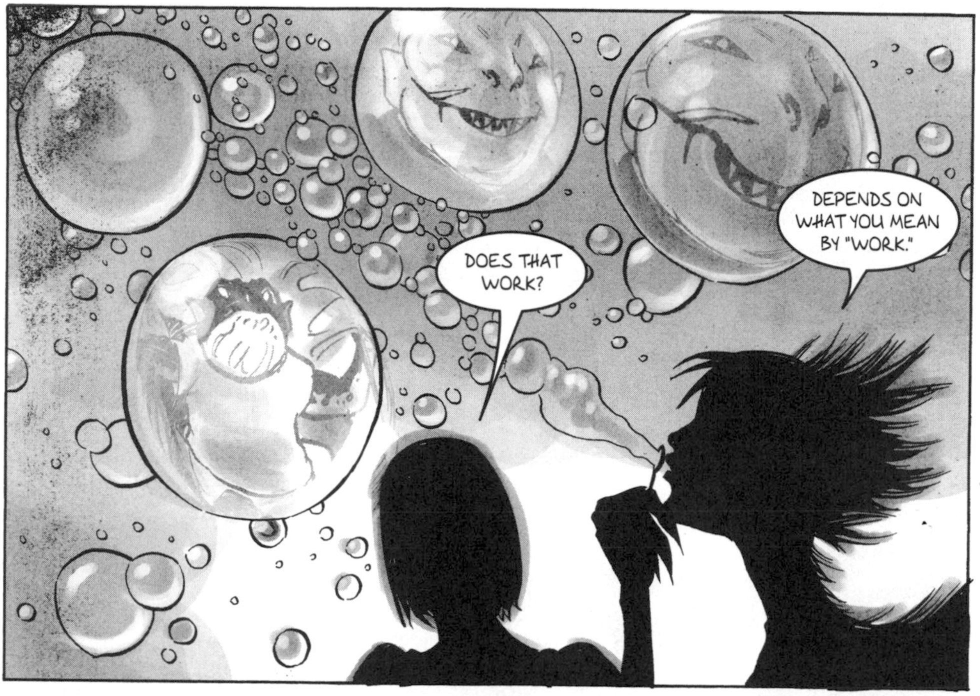
DOES THAT WORK?
DEPENDS ON WHAT YOU MEAN BY "WORK."

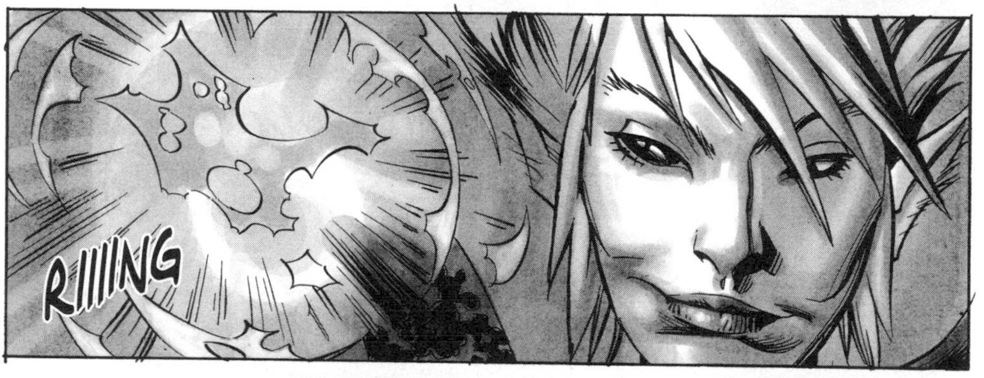
RIIIING

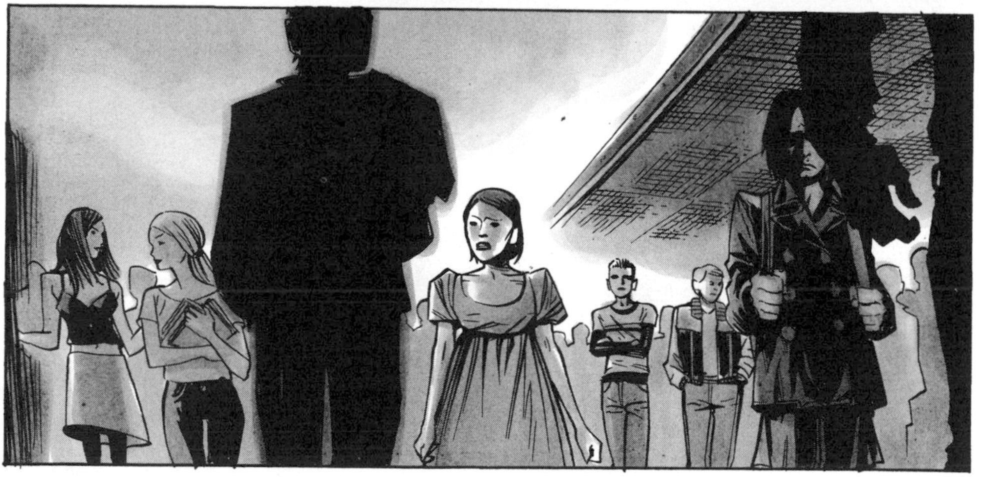

THEY'RE WAITING FOR US AT THE COURT HOUSE.

WHO?

YOUR MOTHER'S FAMILY.

MY MOTHER'S FAMILY? I DIDN'T KNOW MY MOTHER HAD ... FAMILY. WHERE'S DAD?

BEING ARRAIGNED. HE'S FINE.

YOUR MOTHER'S FATHER'S HERE. HE SAYS HE WANTS YOU TO COME AND LIVE WITH HIM. THAT WOULD BE A VERY BAD IDEA, RUE.

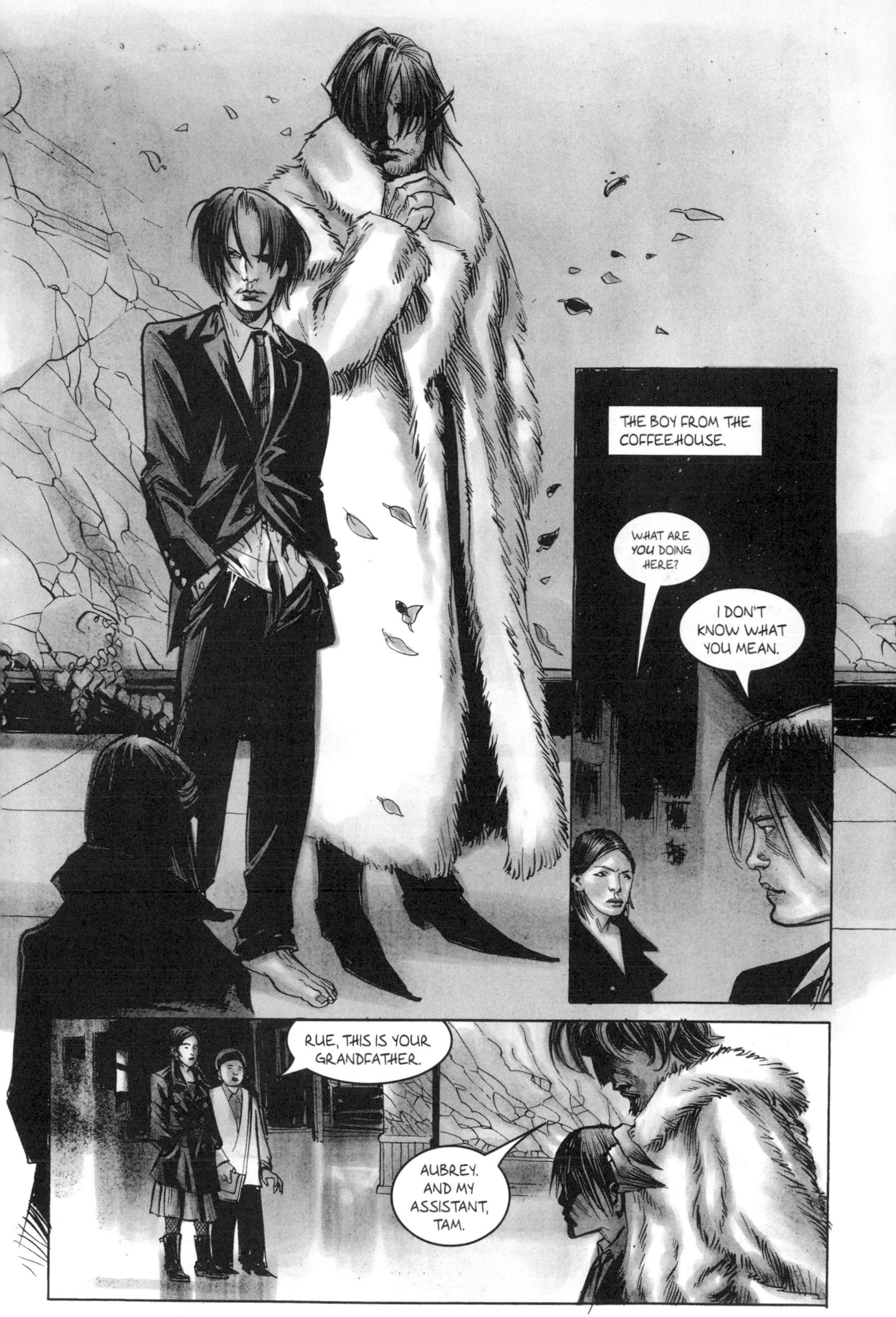
THE BOY FROM THE COFFEEHOUSE.
WHAT ARE YOU DOING HERE?
I DON'T KNOW WHAT YOU MEAN.
RUE, THIS IS YOUR GRANDFATHER.
AUBREY. AND MY ASSISTANT, TAM.

I'VE HEARD SO VERY MUCH ABOUT YOU FROM NIA. YOU ARE RATHER MORE THAN THE CHARMING CHILD I ENVISIONED.

DO YOU KNOW WHERE SHE WENT? MY MOTHER? DID SOMETHING HAPPEN TO HER?

OVER THE RIVER AND THROUGH THE WOODS.

CONTROL THAT, TAM.

SORRY. I'M FINE NOW.

I'M WORRIED ABOUT YOUR MOTHER. THAT'S WHY I CAME FOR YOU.

IT'S TIME YOU MET YOUR TRUE FAMILY.

HER FATHER WILL HOPEFULLY BE OUT ON BAIL TODAY.

THE SAME MAN WHO'S BEING CHARGED WITH THE MURDER OF ONE OF HIS STUDENTS? WHAT AN EXCELLENT IDEA TO LET HIM CARE FOR RUE AS WELL.

I'M NOT GOING ANYWHERE.

HOW DO I KNOW YOU'RE MY GRANDFATHER? I'VE NEVER EVEN SEEN YOU BEFORE.

BUT YOUR FATHER HAS. AND SO HAS SHE. ISN'T THAT RIGHT, MS. VALIA?

YOU'VE MET HIM BEFORE?

IT WAS A LONG TIME AGO.

I'VE FILED PAPERWORK FOR TEMPORARY CUSTODY. WE SHOULD HAVE A HEARING SOON.

YOU CAN'T DO THIS. YOU KNOW THADDEUS IS INNOCENT.

WE KNOW NO SUCH THING.

THAT'S YOUR LAWYER?

YOU'RE STARTING TO SEE. REALLY SEE. NOW YOU JUST NEED TO LOOK.

WHAT IS THAT SUPPOSED TO MEAN?

IT'S TIME FOR US TO GO, I'M AFRAID. COME.

I'M NOT GOING ANYWHERE WITH YOU. ANY OF YOU!

THE LIBRARY WAS A GREAT COMFORT TO ME WHEN I WAS LITTLE.

THE THING ABOUT A MOM LIKE MINE IS THAT SHE NEVER REALLY UNDERSTOOD HOW TO GIVE ADVICE.

MOM...?

THE KIDS AT SCHOOL LAUGHED WHEN I SAID THAT TREES HAVE THEIR OWN LANGUAGE. AND THE SCIENCE TEACHER SAID —

OH, IT'S SO NICE THAT YOU MADE THEM LAUGH!

IF YOU'RE VERY QUIET, YOU CAN HEAR THE WILLOWS GOSSIPING RIGHT NOW, THE WICKED THINGS. HEAR THEM?

BOOKS GAVE BETTER ADVICE. MOSTLY.

I COULD REALLY USE SOME ADVICE RIGHT ABOUT NOW.

44

I WANTED TO SEE FOR MYSELF.

A student of Benton College was found dead this morning, after being missing for more than three days. Sarasa Narayan, 19, was last seen by classmates in her Intro to Folklore class in Morton Hall.

Professor Thaddeus Silver has been charged with her murder. Silver is also being questioned in connection with the disappearance of his wife, Nia, 37.

INSTANT MESSAGE

DEVILDALE: r u there?
DEVILDALE: r u there?
DEVILDALE: r u there?

INTERESTS
swimming, flying, travel.

INSTANT MESSAGE

DEVILDALE: r u there?
DEVILDALE: r u there?
DEVILDALE: r u there?
DEVILDALE: r u there?
DEVILDALE: r u there?
DEVILDALE: r u there?

I HAVEN'T USED A CARD CATALOG IN YEARS.

FAERIE

I'M NOT EVEN SURE WHAT I'M LOOKING FOR.

CAN I HELP YOU FIND SOMETHING?

NO.

TIPPERARY, IRELAND, 1895.

BRIDGET CLEARY WAS FOND OF TAKING LONG WALKS IN THE COUNTRY. HER HUSBAND, MICHAEL, BELIEVED THAT ON ONE OF HER WALKS SHE'D BEEN REPLACED WITH A FAERIE CHANGELING.

SHE'S GROWN TWO INCHES TALLER OVERNIGHT. AND SHE'S... SHE'S TOO SURE OF HERSELF. NOT LIKE OUR BRIDGET.

SHE'S SICKLY, MICHAEL. IT'S THE FEVER.

WHAT'S WRONG WITH YOU? HAVE YOU ALL GONE MAD?

DRINK THIS, WITCH.

ARE YOU BRIDGET BOLAND, WIFE OF MICHAEL CLEARY, IN THE NAME OF GOD?

YES... YES. YOU KNOW I AM.

THEN SWEAR IT. SAY THE WORDS.

I...AM BRIDGET...OH, FATHER, WHAT'S HAPPENING? WHY WON'T YOU TELL HIM WHO I AM?

JUST SAY THE WORDS, BRIDGET.

I'M NO FAERY, MICHAEL! STOP THIS!

DON'T BE AFRAID. JUST SAY, "IN THE NAME OF GOD, I AM BRIDGET BOLAND, WIFE OF MICHAEL BOLAND."

BUT YOU KNOW WHO I AM!

MICHAEL...

PLEASE, BRIDGET. I'M BEGGING YOU.

PUT HER IN THE FIRE!

AAAAAAAUGH!

BRIDGET'S GOING TO RIDE HERE ON A GREY HORSE, BOUND WITH FAERY ROPES AND I NEED TO BE SURE TO CUT HER DOWN. WE'LL ONLY HAVE ONE CHANCE.

THAT'S NOT BRIDGET. DON'T BE FOOLED.

WHAT HAVE YOU DONE?

WHAT PEOPLE WERE MOST SHOCKED BY WAS THAT ANYONE IN 1894 COULD STILL BELIEVE IN FAERIES.

HERE ARE SOME HYPOTHESES I WANT TO TEST:

(A) MY FATHER HAD AN AFFAIR WITH HIS STUDENT AND MY CRAZY MOTHER FOUND OUT AND KILLED THE GIRL IN A JEALOUS RAGE.

(B) MY FATHER HAD AN AFFAIR WITH HIS STUDENT AND MY MOTHER FOUND OUT; DAD KILLED MOM AND THEN THE GIRL.

(C) MY MOTHER WAS STOLEN BY FAERIES THREE WEEKS AGO; THE DEAD GIRL HAS NOTHING TO DO WITH IT.

(D) MY FATHER THOUGHT MY MOTHER WAS A FAERY CHANGELING AND KILLED HER THINKING THAT WOULD BRING MY REAL MOTHER BACK, BUT SHE WASN'T AND NOW SHE'S DEAD; THE DEAD GIRL STILL HAS NOTHING TO DO WITH IT.

MEET ME BY THE MORTON BUILDING, OKAY?

HEY.

I JUST WANT YOU TO KNOW THAT NONE OF US THINK YOUR DAD DID ANYTHING WRONG.

I ONCE SAW YOUR DAD CATCH A SPIDER AND PUT IT OUTSIDE INSTEAD OF STOMPING IT.

HE'S NO KILLER.

NOT THAT THAT MAKES ME LESS OF AN ASS.

I'M SORRY, RUE. HONEST.

EVERYONE SAYS THE SAME THINGS ABOUT KILLERS: "HE WAS SO NICE. HE MOWED THAT OLD LADY'S LAWN FOR NOTHING, TOOK AN OLD 80 POUND BAG OF QUICKLIME OFF MY HANDS."

YOU DON'T THINK YOUR DAD DID IT, DO YOU?

THIS IS WHERE THE GIRL WAS LAST. WE'RE USED TO CREEPING AROUND PLACES. MAYBE WE CAN FIND SOMETHING.

THERE'S NOT GOING TO BE ANYTHING THE POLICE HAVEN'T ALREADY GOT.

COME ON. IF IT WAS MY DAD, I'D WANT TO DO SOMETHING, TOO. CUT SOME SLACK.

HAVE YOU NOTICED THE VINES AROUND HERE ARE GOING CRAZY? I HEARD SOMETHING ON THE NEWS. POISON IVY IS BIGGER AND DEADLIER BECAUSE OF GLOBAL WARMING AND--

SHHHH!

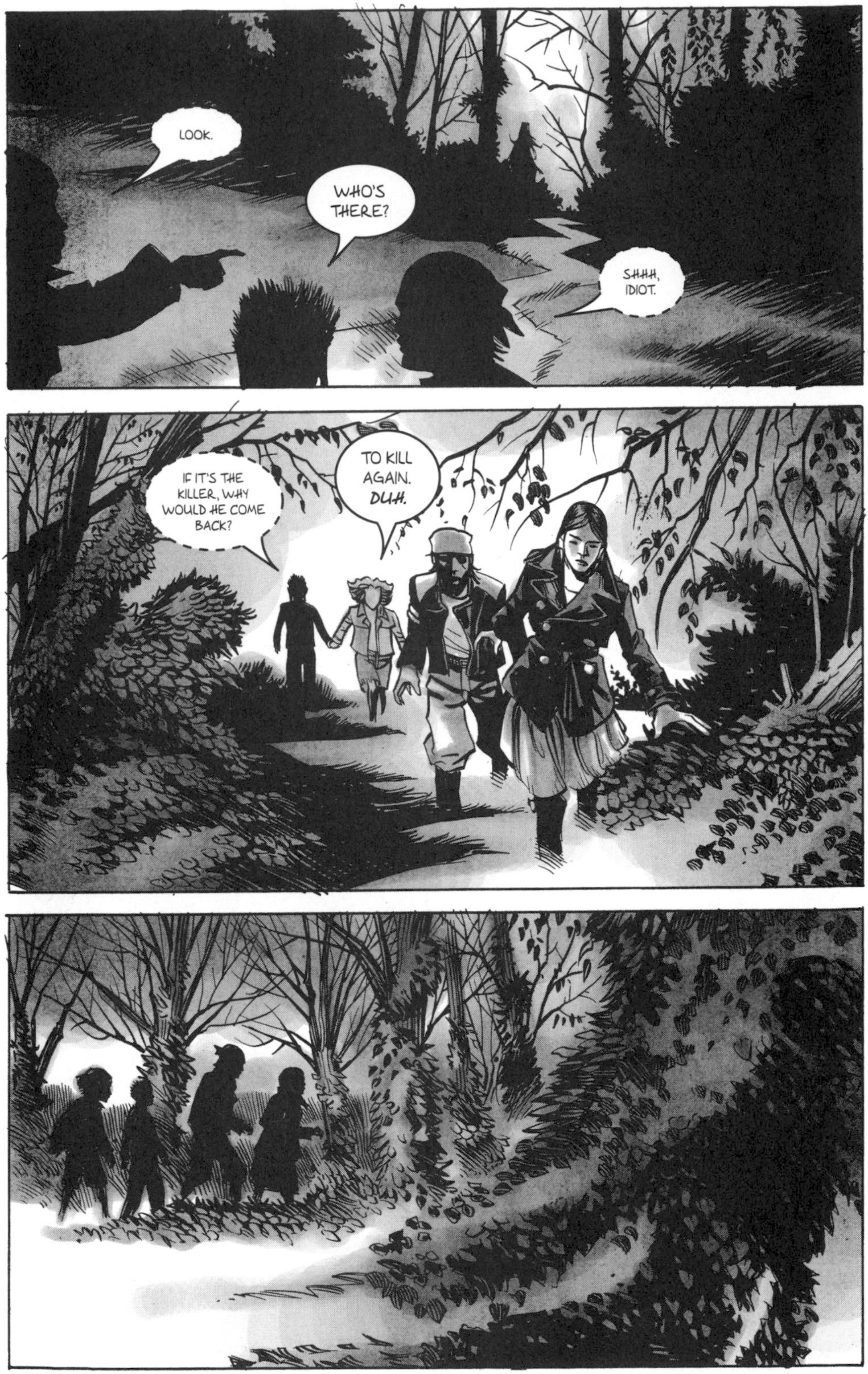
LOOK.
WHO'S THERE?
SHHH, IDIOT.
IF IT'S THE KILLER, WHY WOULD HE COME BACK?
TO KILL AGAIN. DUH.

DO YOU THINK THIS COULD BE A CLUE?

WAIT! WHAT ARE YOU?

AAAAUGH!

THEN THE SHADOW IS GONE AND I'M FALLING.

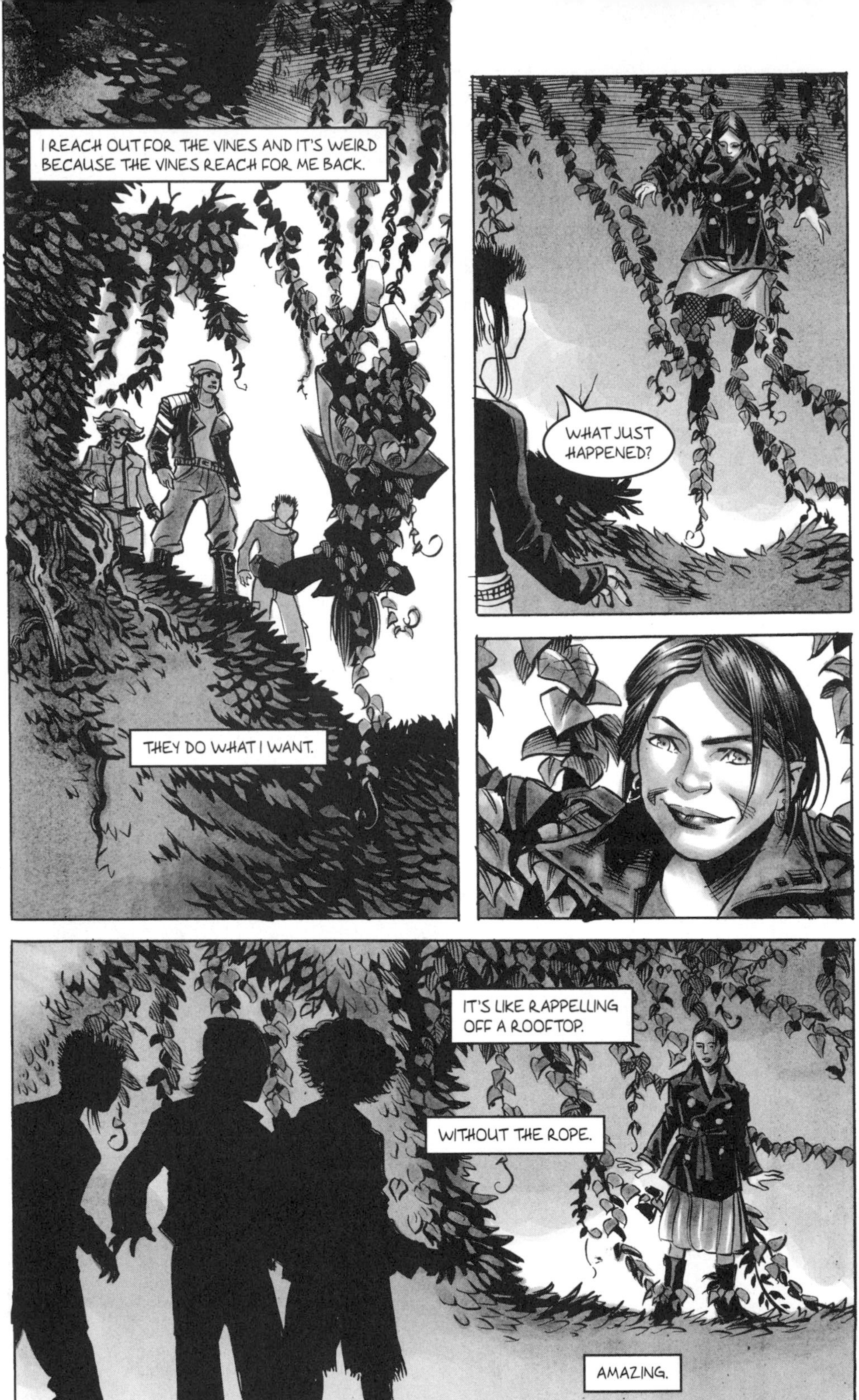
I REACH OUT FOR THE VINES AND IT'S WEIRD BECAUSE THE VINES REACH FOR ME BACK.
THEY DO WHAT I WANT.
WHAT JUST HAPPENED?
IT'S LIKE RAPPELLING OFF A ROOFTOP.
WITHOUT THE ROPE.
AMAZING.

I THINK ABOUT MY MOTHER'S GARDEN.

MOM!

MRS. TANNER'S GOING TO SEE YOU.

PUT ON SOME CLOTHES.

YOUR FATHER SAID THAT I COULD WEAR WHAT I WANTED AT OUR HOUSE.

I THINK HE MEANT *INSIDE* THE HOUSE.

STOP MAKING THE PLANTS DO THAT. IT'S NOT FUNNY. IT'S WORSE THAN BEING NAKED.

YOU WANT TO TELL US WHAT JUST HAPPENED?

I DON'T REMEMBER WHEN I REALIZED MY MOTHER WAS CRAZY. I MUST HAVE BEEN PRETTY YOUNG.

ONLY CRAZY PEOPLE HEAR VOICES. ONLY CRAZY PEOPLE SEE THINGS THAT AREN'T REAL.

AND IF SOMETIMES I THOUGHT I HEARD THINGS OR SAW THINGS TOO, THEN THE DIFFERENCE BETWEEN ME AND MY MOTHER WAS THAT I KNEW IT WAS CRAZY.

BUT NOW THE WHOLE WORLD HAS GONE CRAZY.

I HAVE SOMETHING YOU NEED TO SEE.

HOW ABOUT WE RELOCATE TO SOMEWHERE LESS TERRIFYING FIRST?

LOOK AT WHAT I FOUND.

Please See Me After Class, Prof. Silver

IT DOESN'T MEAN ANYTHING.

WHO'S THERE?

SCATTER AND HIDE.

I'M VERY SORRY TO STARTLE YOU.

I DON'T TRUST YOU. OR AUBREY. YOU CAN TELL HIM SO.

GOOD.

BUT I'M NOT HERE FOR AUBREY.

STALKING ME, TAM?

I'M CURSED. SOMETIMES I SAY TRUE THINGS, THINGS MY CURSE KNOWS BUT I DON'T. USUALLY WHEN I'M ASKED A QUESTION.

SOMETIMES I DON'T EVEN REMEMBER WHAT I SAID.

RUE? WHERE ARE YOU? COME OUT COME OUT WHEREVER YOU ARE.

THAT'S MY CUE. SORRY ABOUT YOUR—

LISTEN. AUBREY ASKED IF ANYONE COULD STOP HIM. I SAID, "ONLY YOUR OWN FLESH CAN STOP YOU," BUT I DON'T KNOW WHY I SAID IT.

HE THINKS IT MEANS YOU.

LISTEN TO ME!

GET OFF ME!

I DON'T UNDERSTAND ANYTHING YOU'VE SAID. STOP WHAT? WHY TELL ME THIS?

BECAUSE I ALSO THINK IT MEANS YOU.

AAAUGH! WHAT—

WHAT AM I SUPPOSED TO STOP?

THE CITY IS
FALLING.

RUE!
WHERE *ARE*
YOU?

I REALLY
HAVE TO
GO.

BYE.

WE WERE
WORRIED.

HERE
I AM.

THERE'S SOMETHING WRONG WITH THIS TOWN.

WHEN DID IT START?

HOW LONG HAVE I NOT BEEN NOTICING?

IT STARTED JUST AFTER MOM DISAPPEARED. MOSTLY IT'S PEOPLE THAT I SEE LOOKING DIFFERENT. LEAF-PATTERNS ON THEIR SKIN, HORNS ON THEIR HEADS. SOMETIMES THEY'RE COVERED IN FUR. THEN I'LL LOOK BACK AND THEY'RE FINE. REGULAR LOOKING.

BUT THEY'RE NOT. THEY'RE FAERIES.

I BELIEVE YOU.

YOU DO? I DON'T WANT TO BE MEAN, BUT STRESS SOMETIMES DOES WEIRD THINGS TO PEOPLE. AND SHE'S BEEN STRESSED.

DON'T BE TOTAL CLOWNS. YOU SAW THE VINES CATCH HER.

THIS IS THE PART IN THE MOVIE WHERE THAT GUY SAYS, "ZOMBIES? WHAT ZOMBIES?" JUST BEFORE THEY EAT HIS BRAINS.

I DON'T WANT TO BE THAT GUY.

WHAT ABOUT YOU, DALE?

I DON'T KNOW.

I'M SORRY.

I JUST DON'T KNOW.

I COULDN'T DESCRIBE DALE'S EXPRESSION, BUT I'D SEEN IT BEFORE.

ON MY FATHER'S FACE, WHEN HE LOOKED AT MY MOTHER.

SO, WHAT DOES THIS HAVE TO DO WITH YOUR DAD?

DUDE, YOU WANT SOME COFFEE WITH YOUR SUGAR?

I CAN'T TELL THEM THAT I'M WONDERING IF MY MOM IS A FAERY. THAT WOULD BE CRAZY.

I DON'T KNOW. I STILL HAVE TO FIGURE THAT PART OUT.

NOTHING'S GOING TO CHANGE BETWEEN US, NO MATTER WHAT.

COME IN FOR A SEC. MY DAD'S NOT HOME, AFTER ALL.

WHAT ABOUT *THEM?*

WE'LL BE QUICK.

RUE?

OH.

HI.

I TALKED TO THE LAWYERS. THEY WERE OPTIMISTIC.

THEY FOUND SOME OF YOUR FATHER'S DNA ON SARASA'S CLOTHING, WHICH IS BAD, BUT HE SAYS THAT HE SPOKE WITH HER BRIEFLY AFTER CLASS. MAYBE HE SNEEZED.

PLENTY OF PEOPLE CAN CONFIRM YOUR FATHER WAS AT A FACULTY MEETING. THERE WAS NO TIME FOR HIM TO LURE HER INTO THE WOODS AND—

THANKS FOR DOING ALL OF THIS. I MEAN, YOU'VE REALLY BEEN INCREDIBLE.

AS FOR YOUR MOTHER, ALL THE EVIDENCE IS CIRCUMSTANTIAL. THEY CAN'T BRING CHARGES.

HE LOOKS SO NORMAL IN THE PICTURE. LIKE THE GUY WHO PICKED OUT ALL THE LIMA BEANS FROM MY SUCCOTASH AND LIFTED ME UP TO CLIMB MY FIRST TREE.

I THINK I'M GOING TO BED.

66

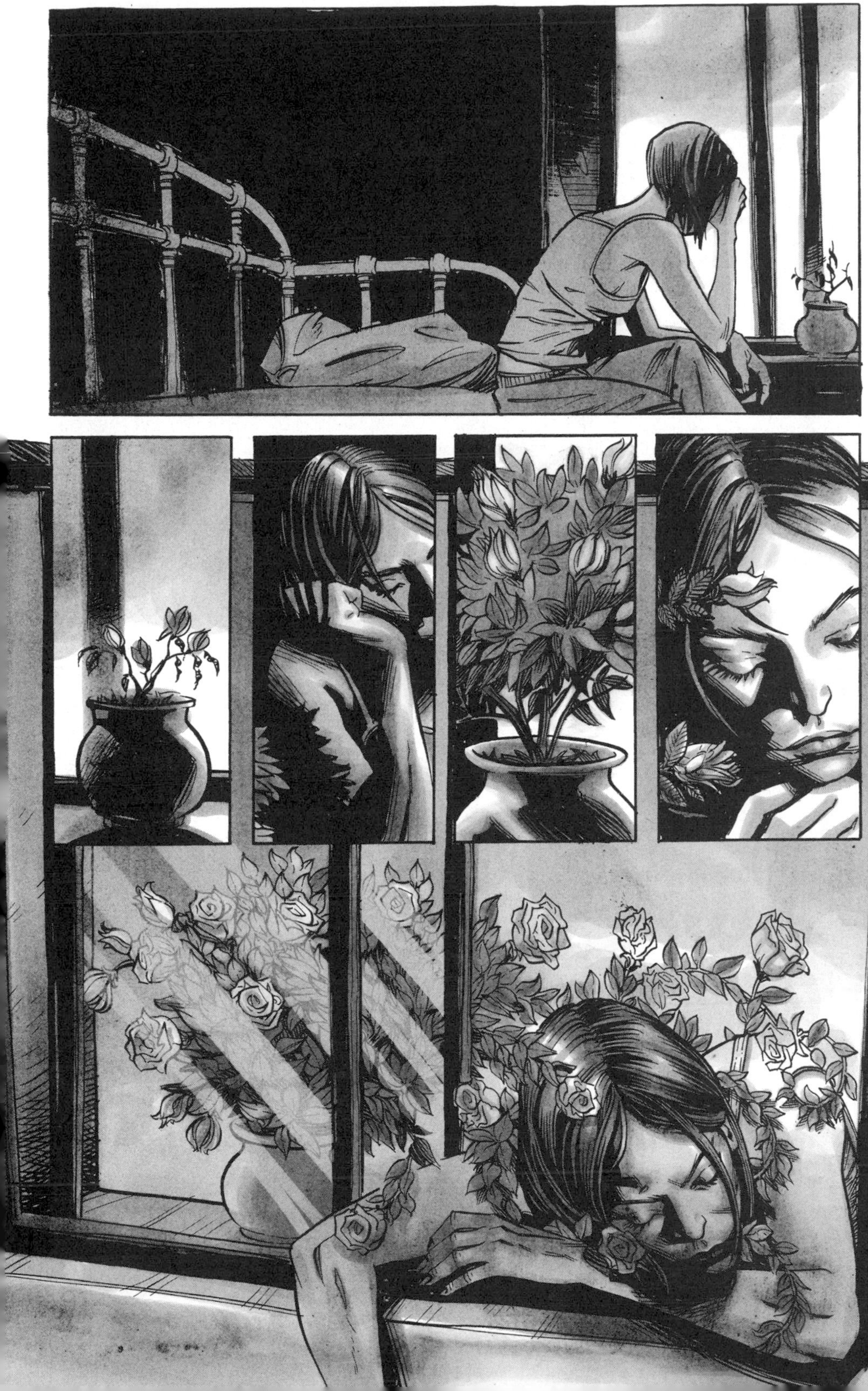

I DON'T KNOW WHAT I'M HOPING TO FIND.

SOMETHING.

SOMETHING THAT WILL PROVE THAT HE DIDN'T DO IT.

PROVE IT TO ME, AT LEAST.

Nancy & Larrise

KNOCK KNOCK

NANCY, RIGHT?

I KNOW THIS IS WEIRD, BUT DO YOU HAVE A MINUTE?

SARASA WAS COOL. DIDN'T BORROW MY CLOTHES WITHOUT ASKING OR DRINK ALL THE MILK.

DIDN'T HAVE A STICK UP HER ASS LIKE HER BROTHER, EITHER.

HER BROTHER?

NAVEEN. HE GOES TO SCHOOL HERE, TOO.

SO THIS IS FOR SOME KIND OF ARTICLE FOR THE NEWSPAPER?

MAYBE. IF I'M LUCKY. SOME INTERNS GET THEIR ARTICLES PUBLISHED.

IT'S SO WEIRD TO THINK THAT SHE'S DEAD.

IS HER BROTHER PICKING ALL THIS STUFF UP?

HE WAS SUPPOSED TO, BUT I HAVEN'T SEEN HIM IN A COUPLE OF DAYS. MAYBE HE'S NOT READY.

I COULD TAKE THEM OVER, IF YOU WANT.

I HAVE TO ASK HIM SOME QUESTIONS.

SURE.

SO WHY DID NAVEEN HAVE A STICK UP HIS ASS?

HE HATED HER BOYFRIEND, WES. ALWAYS CHECKING UP ON HER TO MAKE SURE THAT SHE WASN'T OUT WITH HIM.

REAL UPTIGHT.

10

ARE YOU GOING TO ASK ME ABOUT HER CREEPY PROFESSOR?

RIGHT. UH. WHAT DO YOU KNOW ABOUT HIM?

NOT MUCH. SARASA SAID THAT HE WAS HER FAVORITE TEACHER. THEN TO FIND OUT HE KILLED HER—

IT'S TERRIFYING.

YEAH. PRETTY SCARY.

WHO WERE YOU, SARASA NARAYAN?

WHY DID YOU DIE?

WHO WOULD WANT YOU DEAD?

FOR ONCE, I'M NOT THE ONLY ONE PRETENDING EVERYTHING'S OKAY.

HE-E-EY GIRL, YOU CUT ME LIKE A RA-A-A-ZOR. YOU GU-UT ME, CU-UT ME, GU-UT ME, CU-UT ME.

NOW I KNOW THE LOOK.

HE'S AFRAID.

OF ME.

THANKS FOR COMING. GOOD NIGHT, EVERYONE!

YOU WERE REALLY WONDERFUL.

MY SISTERS AND I LIKE TO SING.

WOULD YOU LIKE TO HEAR US?

UH... YEAH.

HEY! YOU WERE GREAT TONIGHT.

DALE? EVERYTHING OKAY?

SURE.

WHO ARE THE SKANKS?

I JUST REMEMBERED THAT I PROMISED MY MOTHER I'D BE HOME EARLY TONIGHT.

CATCH UP WITH YOU GUYS LATER.

DALE!

LOSE SOMETHING?

I DON'T HAVE TIME FOR THIS RIGHT NOW.

FOR A MOMENT, I THOUGHT HE WAS GOING TO KISS ME.

HOW SICK IS THAT?

FORGIVE ME. THIS TIME I AM HERE FOR AUBREY.

I WONDER IF AUBREY IS REALLY MY GRANDFATHER.

I THINK ABOUT BRIDGET CLEARY. I THINK ABOUT HOW WE ALL THINK WE'RE SAFE WITH OUR FAMILIES.

UNTIL WE'RE NOT.

WAKE UP, LITTLE GIRL.

GET AWAY FROM ME!

IF YOU WISH IT.

LET ME TELL YOU A STORY. THAT'S WHAT GRANDFATHERS DO WHEN LITTLE GIRLS ARE IN BED, ISN'T IT?

LONG AGO, MORTALS CALLED US THE FAIR FOLK, THE PEOPLE OF PEACE, THE GOOD NEIGHBORS.

THEY CALLED US THESE THINGS NOT BECAUSE WE WERE FAIR OR PEACEFUL OR GOOD, BUT BECAUSE THEY FEARED US.

AS THEY SHOULD.

AS THEY WILL AGAIN.

SO WHAT DO YOU WANT WITH ME?

HAVE THEY BRED ALL OF THE ENCHANTMENT OUT OF YOU? AND TRAINED YOU SO THAT YOU HAVE NO CONCERN FOR YOUR OWN KIND?

IS THAT WHAT MY DAUGHTER CHOSE FOR HER OWN DAUGHTER?

WHERE'S MY MOTHER?

WHY DON'T YOU ASK THADDEUS?

IF HE REALLY MURDERED MY MOTHER, YOU WOULDN'T BE IMPLYING IT TO ME. YOU WOULDN'T BE CRYPTIC.

YOU DON'T SEEM THAT NICE A GUY.

WELL SPOTTED.

INDEED, I TAKE NO PLEASURE IN NICETIES.

AND I'M THINKING THAT IF MY DAD REALLY KILLED MY MOM, YOU WOULD HAVE DONE SOMETHING NOT NICE TO HIM ALREADY.

PERHAPS YOU AREN'T HOPELESS AFTER ALL.

LET ME GIVE YOU A CHOICE FOR YOUR CLEVERNESS. YOU CAN GO HOME TO A MOTHER AND FATHER AND HAVE THINGS THE WAY THEY WERE... OR YOU CAN EMBRACE YOUR BIRTHRIGHT.

YOU'RE ONE OF US.

INHUMAN. FEY.

BE ONE OF US.

A LOT OF KIDS HAVE THIS FANTASY THAT SECRETLY THEY'RE REALLY THE PRINCESS OF A FOREIGN COUNTRY.

TURNS OUT THAT PRETTY MUCH SUCKS.

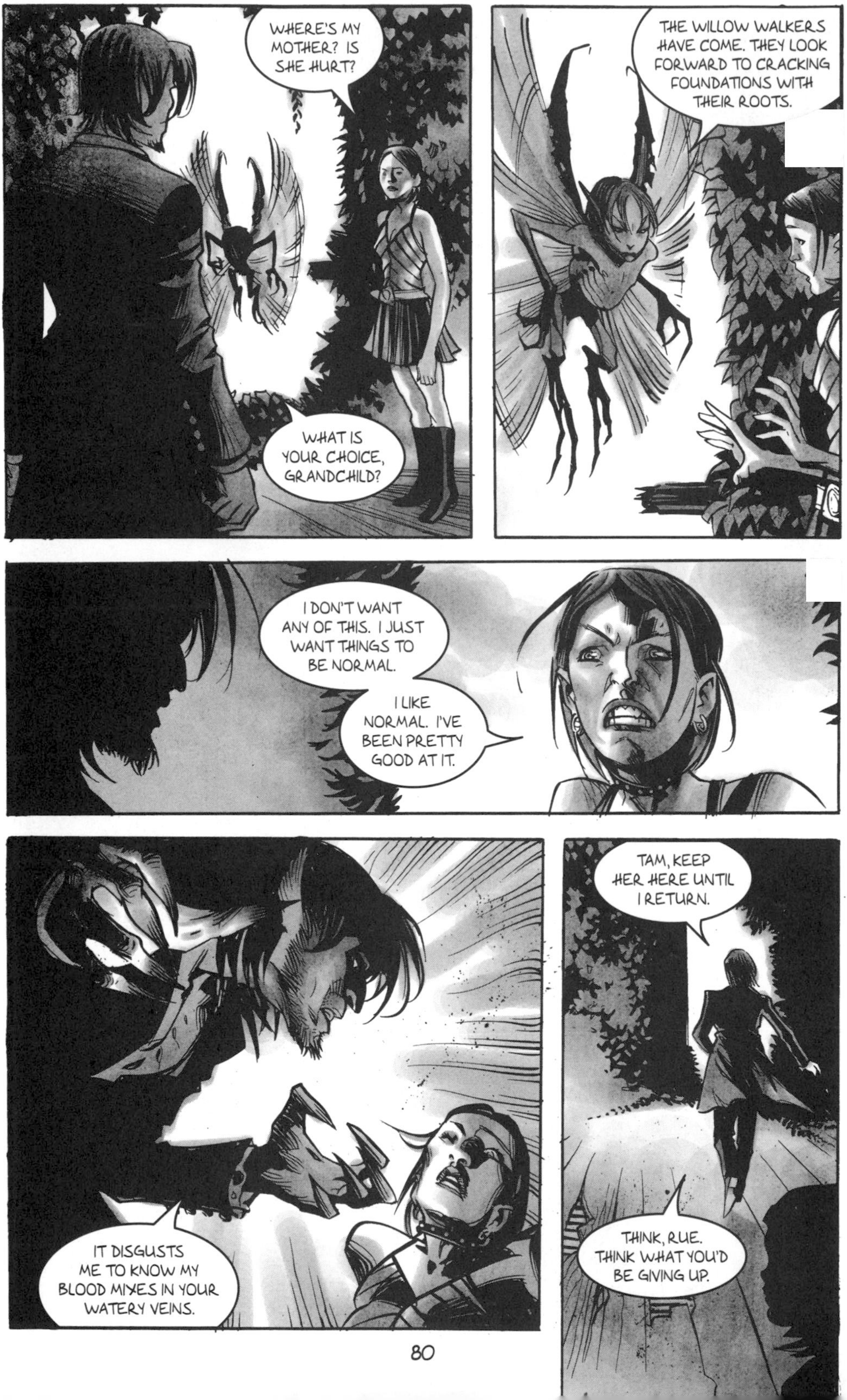
WHERE'S MY MOTHER? IS SHE HURT?
WHAT IS YOUR CHOICE, GRANDCHILD?
THE WILLOW WALKERS HAVE COME. THEY LOOK FORWARD TO CRACKING FOUNDATIONS WITH THEIR ROOTS.
I DON'T WANT ANY OF THIS. I JUST WANT THINGS TO BE NORMAL.
I LIKE NORMAL. I'VE BEEN PRETTY GOOD AT IT.
IT DISGUSTS ME TO KNOW MY BLOOD MIXES IN YOUR WATERY VEINS.
TAM, KEEP HER HERE UNTIL I RETURN.
THINK, RUE. THINK WHAT YOU'D BE GIVING UP.

SOME CHOICE.

SO... I DON'T SUPPOSE I CAN LEAVE?

NO.

PLEEEEEASE?

I'M BOUND TO AUBREY.

HIS WILL COMMANDS ME.

GO.

OKAY.
CAN I GO TO THE
BATHROOM? OR DO
YOU NEED TO WATCH
THAT, TOO?

I THINK ABOUT THE TIMES THAT I CRAWLED DOWN BUILDINGS FOR FUN.

HOW I HID FROM PASSERSBY.

MY HEART BEATS SO HARD IT HURTS.

SORRY I DIDN'T GET HOME LAST NIGHT...

I...

MOM?

DID YOU REALLY THINK I'D JUST LEAVE YOU?

84

WHAT HAPPENED?

I'M SICK, RUE. I'M DYING.

DYING?

IT'S NOT AUBREY'S FAULT.

I'M GLAD YOU GOT TO MEET HIM. HE'S NOT NEARLY AS TERRIBLE AS HE SEEMS.

I FIND THAT HARD TO BELIEVE.

I'LL MEET WITH THE LAWYERS. I'LL MAKE THEM UNDERSTAND.

NOW THAT I'M HERE, EVERYTHING WILL BE OKAY.

I SHOULD JUST GO TO SCHOOL, RIGHT?

OR NOT.

IT'S HARD TO GO FROM BELIEVING YOU'RE CRAZY TO REALIZING THE WHOLE WORLD IS.

HEY EVERYONE! GUESS WHAT? FAERIES ARE REAL! TOTALLY REAL AND ALL AROUND YOU.

YOU KNOW, *FAERIES*. THE LITTLE PEOPLE. THE PEOPLE OF PEACE. THE GOOD NEIGHBORS.

WE'RE GOING TO TAKE OVER YOUR TOWN.

WHAT'S WRONG WITH HER?

SHE THINKS SHE'S A FAIRY.

THAT WENT ABOUT AS WELL AS I EXPECTED.

DON'T SAY I DIDN'T WARN YOU.

SO THEY REALLY CAN'T SEE ME?

NOT IF YOU DON'T WANT THEM TO.

MAYBE I CAN STAY UP HERE FOREVER.

OF COURSE YOU CAN.

FOR A HUNDRED HUNDRED YEARS, IF YOU WANT.

I WANT.

DAD'S LAWYERS SAY THAT MOM TURNING UP MADE THE PROSECUTION'S LAWYERS LOOK STUPID.

IT WAS A PUBLIC RELATIONS NIGHTMARE. SINCE DAD'S ALIBI FOR SARASA'S MURDER SEEMED TO HOLD UP AND MY MOTHER OBVIOUSLY HADN'T BEEN KILLED, THEY HAD TO LET HIM GO. THE MEDIA LOVED IT.

POOF! CHARGES DROPPED.

LIKE IT NEVER HAPPENED.

BUT I STILL WONDER ABOUT SARASA.

IS WES AROUND?

UPSTAIRS.

YOU WANT ME TO COME WITH?

JUST GIVE ME A COUPLE OF MINUTES.

SO, WHAT WAS WITH THOSE GIRLS THE OTHER NIGHT?

DON'T BE LIKE THAT. IT WAS NOTHING.

WES? IS WES IN THERE?

HEY THERE, CUTIE. COME ON AND HAVE A SEAT.

IS THIS YOURS?

I GAVE THAT TO —

YOU KNEW SARASA?

I KEEP PICTURING WHAT HAPPENED. WHO WOULD WANT TO HURT HER?

IT'S TOO LOUD TO TALK IN HERE. COME ON.

I KNOW WHAT IT LOOKS LIKE, ME PARTYING AND EVERYTHING, BUT I LOVED HER. AND I NEVER THOUGHT IT WAS THAT PROFESSOR.

IT WAS HER BROTHER, NAVEEN.

DID YOU TELL THAT TO THE POLICE?

NO. I DIDN'T HAVE ANY PROOF. WHY WOULD THEY BELIEVE ME?

WHY DO *YOU* BELIEVE IT?

HE HATED THAT SARASA LOVED ME.

YOU SHOULD HAVE HEARD THE THINGS HE SAID, THE WAY HE THREATENED ME.

SAID HE'D FEED ME MY BALLS.

BUT I NEVER FIGURED HE'D HURT *HER*.

LOOK, ANY FRIEND OF SARASA'S IS A FRIEND OF MINE. HANG OUT. ENJOY THE PARTY.

JUST STAY AWAY FROM NAVEEN. HE MIGHT COME AROUND HERE LATER.

WHY DO I CARE ABOUT SOME DEAD GIRL WHILE MY OWN MOTHER IS DYING?

WHAT DID HE SAY?

YOU KNOW, THIS IS A GREAT PARTY. {HIC}

LET'S GO, LUSH.

I WAS SO SURPRISED TO SEE YOUR MOTHER TODAY. I THOUGHT SHE WAS MURDERED.

WHAT?

SHE SAID SHE WAS SICK. ARE YOU SURE YOUR FATHER ISN'T POISONING HER SO HE CAN GO OFF WITH THAT DUMPY FRIEND?

I SAW THEM TOGETHER.

DUMPY FRIEND?

NO, MRS. TANNER, I DON'T THINK SO.

OH. WELL, WOULD YOU LIKE A PIECE OF OATCAKE? FRESH BAKED.

THE DOCTORS DON'T KNOW WHAT'S WRONG WITH HER. SHE WON'T LET THEM RUN TESTS.

MOM, WHEN YOU DISAPPEARED — WHAT HAPPENED?

I WENT HOME FOR A WHILE, THAT'S ALL.

YOUR FATHER BROKE A PROMISE.

WHERE'S HOME? WHAT AM I? WHAT ARE YOU?

YOU'RE A FAERY, LIKE ME.

AND WE MUST NEVER REALLY TRUST THE HUMANS. REMEMBER THAT, WHEN I'M GONE.

THAT DOESN'T SOUND LIKE SOMETHING MY MOTHER WOULD SAY.

IT DOESN'T SOUND LIKE HER AT ALL.

MOM?

DO YOU REMEMBER WHEN I DYED MY HAIR BRIGHT BLUE?

THE WORDS JUST FALL FROM MY LIPS.

DAD SAID THAT I LOOKED LIKE A SMURF, BUT YOU SAID I WAS A NYMPH.

I DON'T KNOW WHAT MADE ME THINK OF THAT.

OF COURSE I REMEMBER.

I REMEMBER EVERYTHING I'VE EVER KNOWN OF YOU.

IT WAS LUCY WHO DYED HER HAIR BLUE, NOT ME.

THE GROUT IN THE UPSTAIRS BATHROOM IS STILL STAINED FROM IT.

I LOVE YOU, MOM.

NOW I'M WORRIED.

I CAN'T PRETEND I'M NOT WORRIED.

KNOCK!
KNOCK!

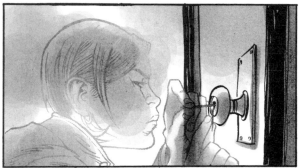

IT'S EASIER TO CREEP AROUND NOW THAT I CAN MAKE MYSELF INVISIBLE.

NOT EXACTLY LIKE BREAKING INTO AN ABANDONED BUILDING.

BUT NOT AS DIFFERENT AS YOU'D FIGURE.

TOO MANY FOR IT TO BE FROM A LEAKY COMFORTER.

NOT THE KIND USED IN PILLOWS. THE LONG ONES.

ALL OF THEM, WHITE AS SNOW.

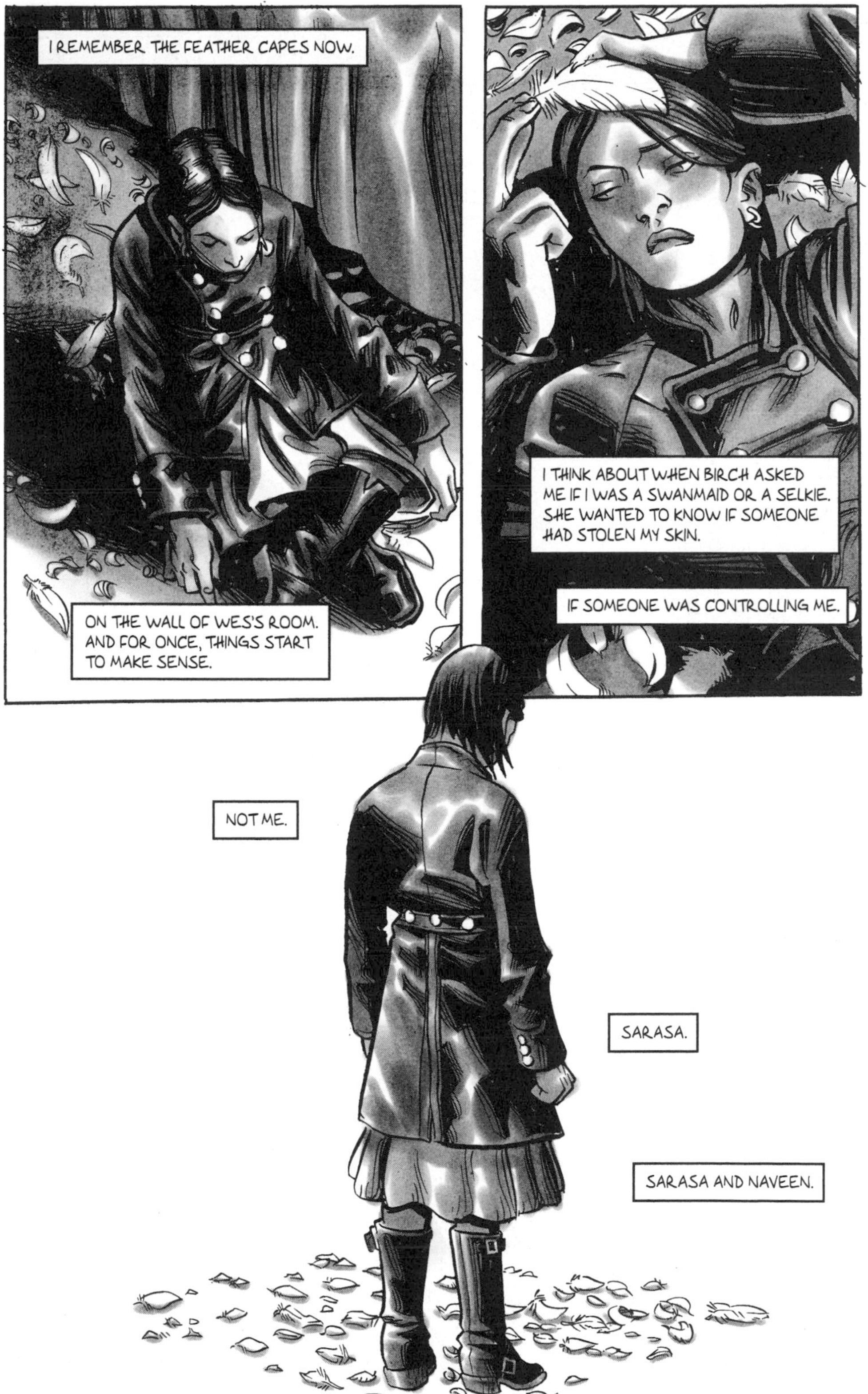
I REMEMBER THE FEATHER CAPES NOW.
ON THE WALL OF WES'S ROOM. AND FOR ONCE, THINGS START TO MAKE SENSE.
I THINK ABOUT WHEN BIRCH ASKED ME IF I WAS A SWANMAID OR A SELKIE. SHE WANTED TO KNOW IF SOMEONE HAD STOLEN MY SKIN.
IF SOMEONE WAS CONTROLLING ME.
NOT ME.
SARASA.
SARASA AND NAVEEN.

I FIND HIM THE FIRST PLACE I LOOK.

YOU'RE NAVEEN, AREN'T YOU? SARASA'S BROTHER.

YOU'RE NOT HUMAN.

NEITHER ARE YOU.

WES HAS YOUR SWAN SKIN, DOESN'T HE? THAT'S WHY YOU COULDN'T STOP HIM FROM KILLING HER, ISN'T IT?

IT'S NOT YOUR FAULT.

IF THAT WAS ALL I DID, IT WOULD BE ENOUGH.

BUT I HAVE DONE MUCH MORE.

100

SINCE WE WERE CHILDREN, WE'VE TRAVELED TOGETHER. NO HOME. NO NEED FOR ONE.

ALL WE NEEDED WAS FREEDOM.

WE THOUGHT IT WOULD BE INTERESTING TO GO TO SCHOOL FOR A TIME.

THERE WERE SO MANY THINGS TO LEARN.

MY SISTER WAS A FLIRT.

SOON SHE HAD – WHAT DO YOU SAY? – BOYS EATING OUT OF HER HANDS.

WES WAS MERELY ONE OF THEM.

THE ONLY DIFFERENCE WAS THAT HE DISCOVERED US.

HIS EYES NEVER LEFT HER.

HE MUST HAVE FOLLOWED US AND GUESSED THE REST.

SHE HAD TO PLAY THE PART OF HIS LOVING SLAVE.

AND I HAD TO LET HER.

WHAT YOU DON'T UNDERSTAND IS HOW MUCH OUR FREEDOM MATTERED.

WE'D RATHER DIE THAN BE CAPTIVES.

IT WILL BE QUICK.

WE DID THE ONLY THING THAT WES HADN'T FORBIDDEN.

THE ONLY THING THAT WOULD FREE US.

SHE MISSED MY HEART.

.SHE MISSED IT BY A MILE.

103

I WENT TO LOCAL FAERIES. BEFORE. THEY WOULDN'T HELP US GET THE SWAN SKINS BACK.

THEY WOULDN'T DO ANYTHING BUT USE SARASA'S DEATH TO CAUSE TROUBLE FOR SOME MORTAL.

WES TOLD US WE COULDN'T KILL OURSELVES. AS LONG AS HE HAS MY CAPE, I MUST OBEY HIM.

BUT YOU COULD. FOR SARASA. AVENGE HER. PLEASE.

NO.

MAYBE I SHOULD FEEL BAD FOR HIM.

I FEEL NOTHING.

YOU CAN ALWAYS COUNT ON YOUR FAMILY TO LOVE YOU.

AND TO BETRAY YOU.

AND THEN TO FEEL GUILTY ABOUT IT.

AMANDA'S BEEN REALLY GOOD TO ME AND DAD.

TOO GOOD. GUILTY GOOD.

DAD'S DUMPY FRIEND, WHO SEEMS VERY DISTRACTED THESE DAYS.

WHAT DID YOU AND MY DAD DO? WHAT DID YOU DO TO MY MOM?

WAIT. YOU DON'T UNDERSTAND.

IT TOOK A WHILE. MRS. TANNER EVEN TOLD ME, BUT I WASN'T LISTENING.

YOU NEVER SAID ANYTHING ABOUT MY MOTHER COMING HOME. YOU DIDN'T TRY AND TALK MY DAD INTO REPORTING HER MISSING.

NOW SHE'S *DYING!* WHAT DID YOU DO TO HER?

IT'S NOT WHAT YOU THINK.

SO YOU DIDN'T HAVE AN AFFAIR WITH MY DAD? YOU DON'T KNOW WHAT HAPPENED TO MY MOM?

GO AHEAD. DENY IT.

I CAN'T.

YOUR DAD AND I MET IN GRAD SCHOOL. WE WERE A PAIR OF PASSIONATE NERDS TALKING ABOUT HEINLEIN AND THE VIABILITY OF POLYAMORY AND WHETHER OR NOT QUANTUM PHYSICS MEANT MAGIC WAS REAL.

I WAS IN LOVE WITH HIM.

I WAS TOO SHY TO TELL HIM. SO I JUST FOLLOWED HIM AROUND, HOPING HE'D NOTICE ME.

LOOK AT THIS? IMAGINE IF YOU REALLY COULD SEE FAERIES LIKE IT SAYS IN THE BOOKS.

IT STARTED LIKE A FOLKLORIST'S VERSION OF BLOODY MARY, BUT INSTEAD OF CHANTING IN FRONT OF A MIRROR AT MIDNIGHT, WE TRIED TO GIVE OURSELVES THE SECOND SIGHT.

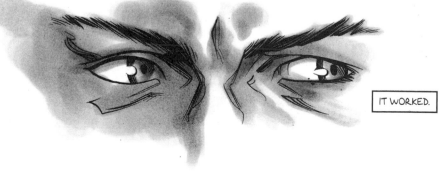

IT WORKED.

IT WAS LIKE A WHOLE NEW WORLD OPENED UP IN FRONT OF OUR EYES.

WE SPIED ON THEM.

YOU KNOW THE WAY FAERIES ARE IN THE FOLKTALES. IF THEY NOTICE US —

I DON'T CARE. I HAD TO SEE HER AGAIN.

I LOVE HER.

YOU DON'T EVEN KNOW HER. YOU PROBABLY HAVE NOTHING IN COMMON.

THERE'S NOTHING COMMON ABOUT HER.

WAIT. EXCUSE ME.

ALLOW ME TO INTRODUCE MYSELF.

I'M THADDEUS. THADDEUS SILVER.

I'M NIA.

HOW COULD HE NOT LOVE HER? SHE WAS PERFECT.

WEREN'T YOU PISSED, THOUGH? I MEAN, HE PICKED HER INSTEAD OF YOU.

I THOUGHT HE WOULD CHANGE HIS MIND.

I THOUGHT THAT MY TRUE FRIENDSHIP WOULD COME TO MEAN MORE TO HIM THAN HER BEAUTY.

I'M SORRY. I DIDN'T KNOW—

THAT SHE WAS MY DAUGHTER? THAT SHE WASN'T JUST SOME MAID YOU COULD STEAL THE SKIN OF AND CARRY OFF?

YOU DARE COURT MY DAUGHTER WITHOUT MY PERMISSION?

I WOULD NEVER DO ANYTHING TO HURT NIA. I LOVE HER.

MORTALS ARE INCONSTANT LOVERS.

MY PERMISSION WAS GIVEN, FATHER. YOURS DOES NOT SUPERCEDE MINE.

VERY WELL, DAUGHTER, LET ME TEST HIM.

PICK MY NIA FROM AMONG HER SISTERS.

IT'S A TRICK!

IF YOU CHOOSE HER, SHE WILL BE YOURS, BUT IF YOU CHOOSE WRONG, YOU MUST LEAVE NOW AND NEVER COME NEAR HER AGAIN.

WHAT DO I DO?

I SHOULD HAVE KEPT MY MOUTH SHUT.

I'D SEEN NIA'S SLIPPERS GET MUDDY DANCING WITH THADDEUS.

MAYBE IT WOULD HAVE BEEN BETTER TO LET HIM FAIL. I COULD HAVE COMFORTED HIM. MAYBE THE COMFORTING WOULD HAVE TURNED INTO SOMETHING ELSE.

LOOK AT THEIR FEET.

THAT'S NIA.

YOU HAVE WON MY DAUGHTER, BUT I SET THIS GEAS UPON YOU — IF YOU ARE EVER UNFAITHFUL TO HER, EVEN FOR A MOMENT, I WILL RIP HER FROM YOUR SIDE.

THERE IS NO ONE ELSE I COULD IMAGINE WANTING.

SO THEY FELL IN LOVE. AND THEY HAD ME. WHAT CHANGED?

WHAT DID YOU DO?

YOU KNOW HOW BEAUTIFUL YOUR MOTHER IS, HOW PERFECT. BUT PERFECTION GROWS FRIGHTENING WITH TIME.

YOUR DAD GOT OLDER, GOT A GUT, AND SILVER HAIR. NIA NEVER GOT PLUMPER OR GRAYER OR ANY DIFFERENT AT ALL. HIS DESIRE FOR HER COOLED AS HIS DISCOMFORT GREW.

HE TOLD YOU ALL THAT?

HE TOLD ME ENOUGH.

RIIIING! RIIIING!

WHAT HAPPENED THEN?

I STILL LOVED HIM, RUE. I TOOK MY CHANCE.

RIIIING! RIIIING!

THADDEUS, WHAT'S WRONG?

I CAN'T BELIEVE I WAS ARGUING WITH AMANDA WHEN MY MOTHER DIED.

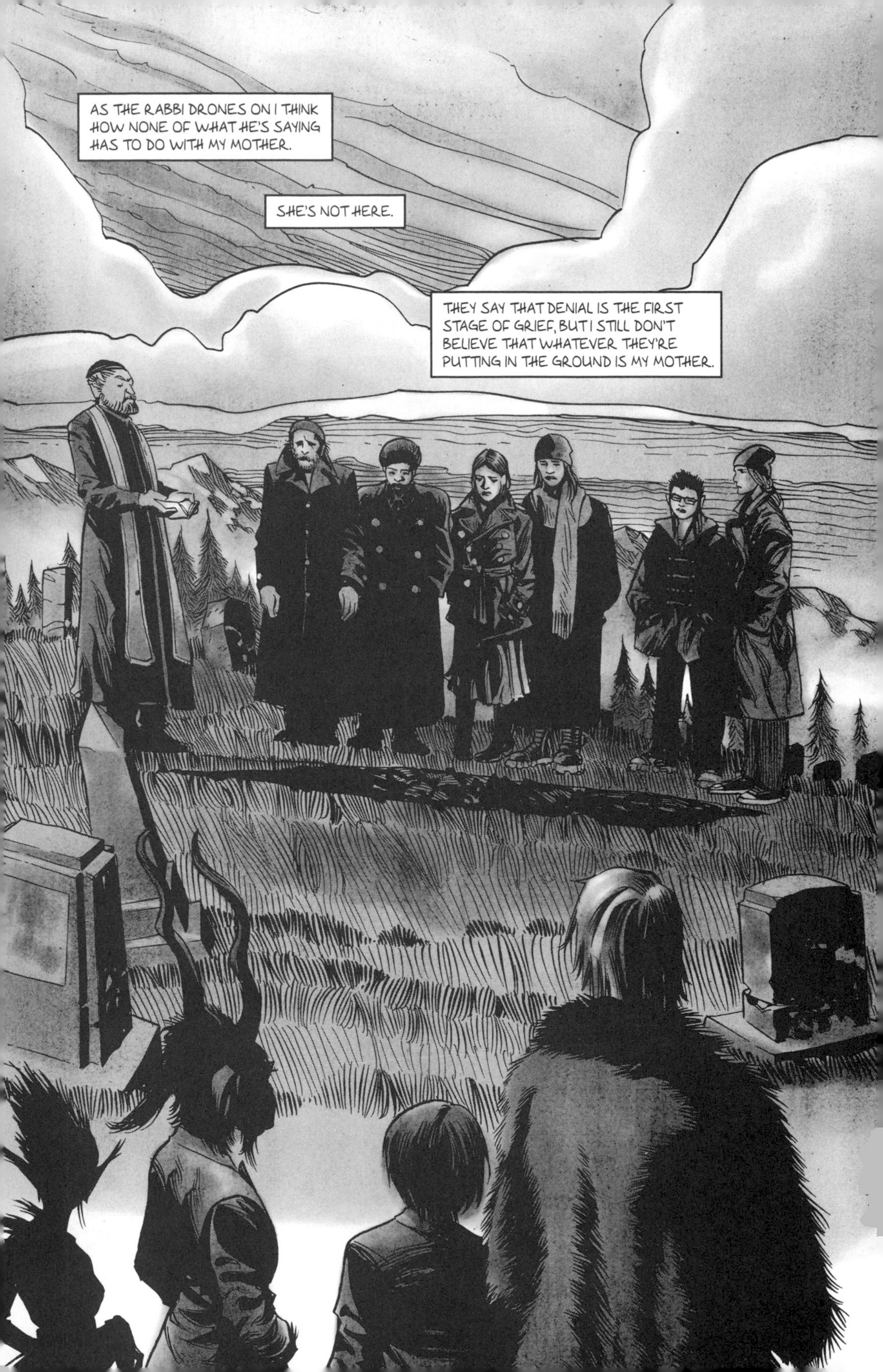
AS THE RABBI DRONES ON I THINK HOW NONE OF WHAT HE'S SAYING HAS TO DO WITH MY MOTHER.
SHE'S NOT HERE.
THEY SAY THAT DENIAL IS THE FIRST STAGE OF GRIEF, BUT I STILL DON'T BELIEVE THAT WHATEVER THEY'RE PUTTING IN THE GROUND IS MY MOTHER.

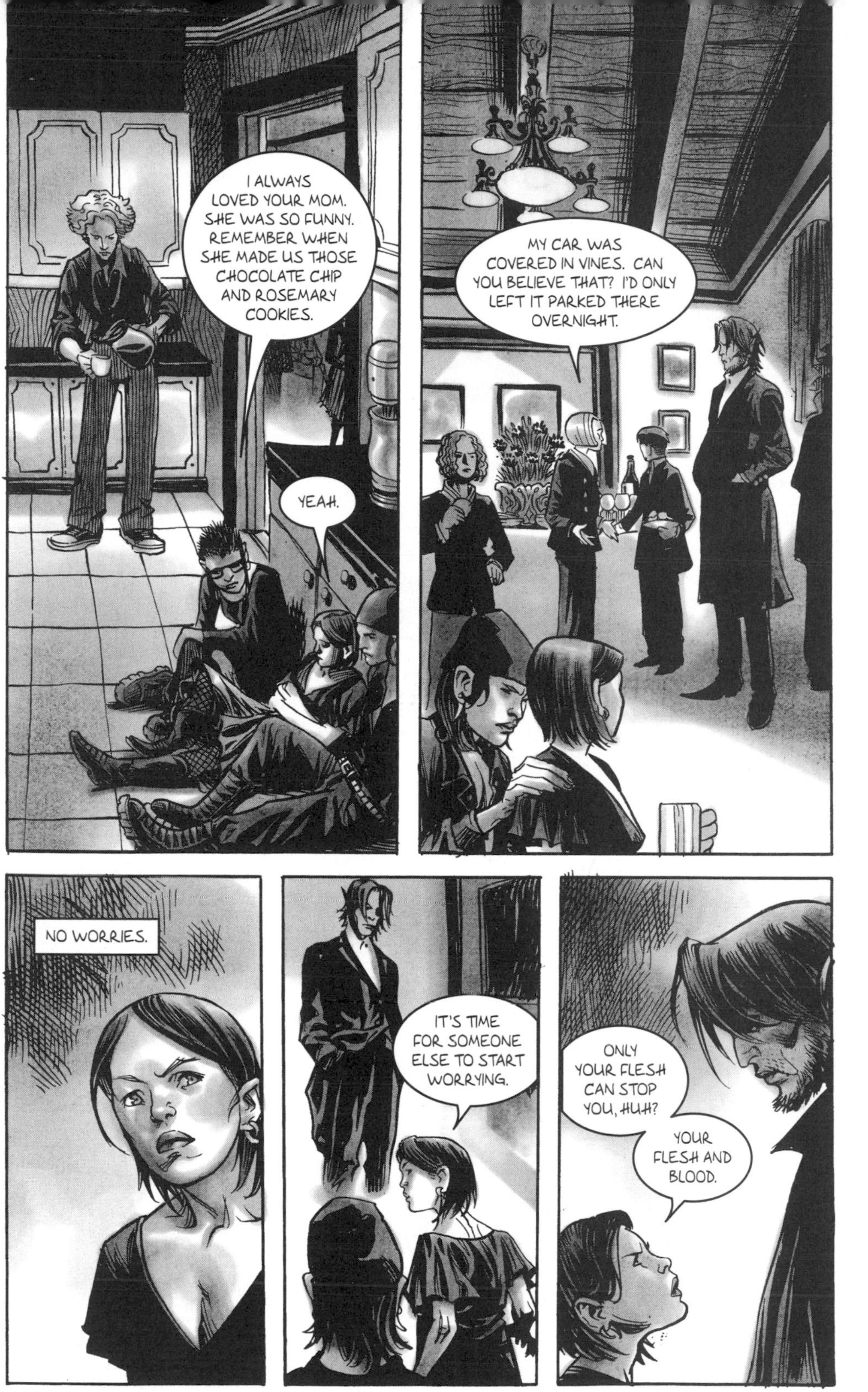
I ALWAYS LOVED YOUR MOM. SHE WAS SO FUNNY. REMEMBER WHEN SHE MADE US THOSE CHOCOLATE CHIP AND ROSEMARY COOKIES.
YEAH.
MY CAR WAS COVERED IN VINES. CAN YOU BELIEVE THAT? I'D ONLY LEFT IT PARKED THERE OVERNIGHT.
NO WORRIES.
IT'S TIME FOR SOMEONE ELSE TO START WORRYING.
ONLY YOUR FLESH CAN STOP YOU, HUH?
YOUR FLESH AND BLOOD.

DALE WOULDN'T COME.

MAYBE HE'S NOT THE GUY I THOUGHT HE WAS.

MAYBE I'M NOT THE GIRL HE THOUGHT I WAS EITHER.

WHAT KIND OF GIRL WOULD DIG UP HER MOM, AFTER ALL?

SHE'S NOT GOING TO RISE UP HUNGERING FOR BRAINS, RIGHT?

JUST DIG.

I JUST HAD TO SEE IF IT WAS REALLY HER IN THERE.

IF THERE'S ANYTHING IN THERE AT ALL.

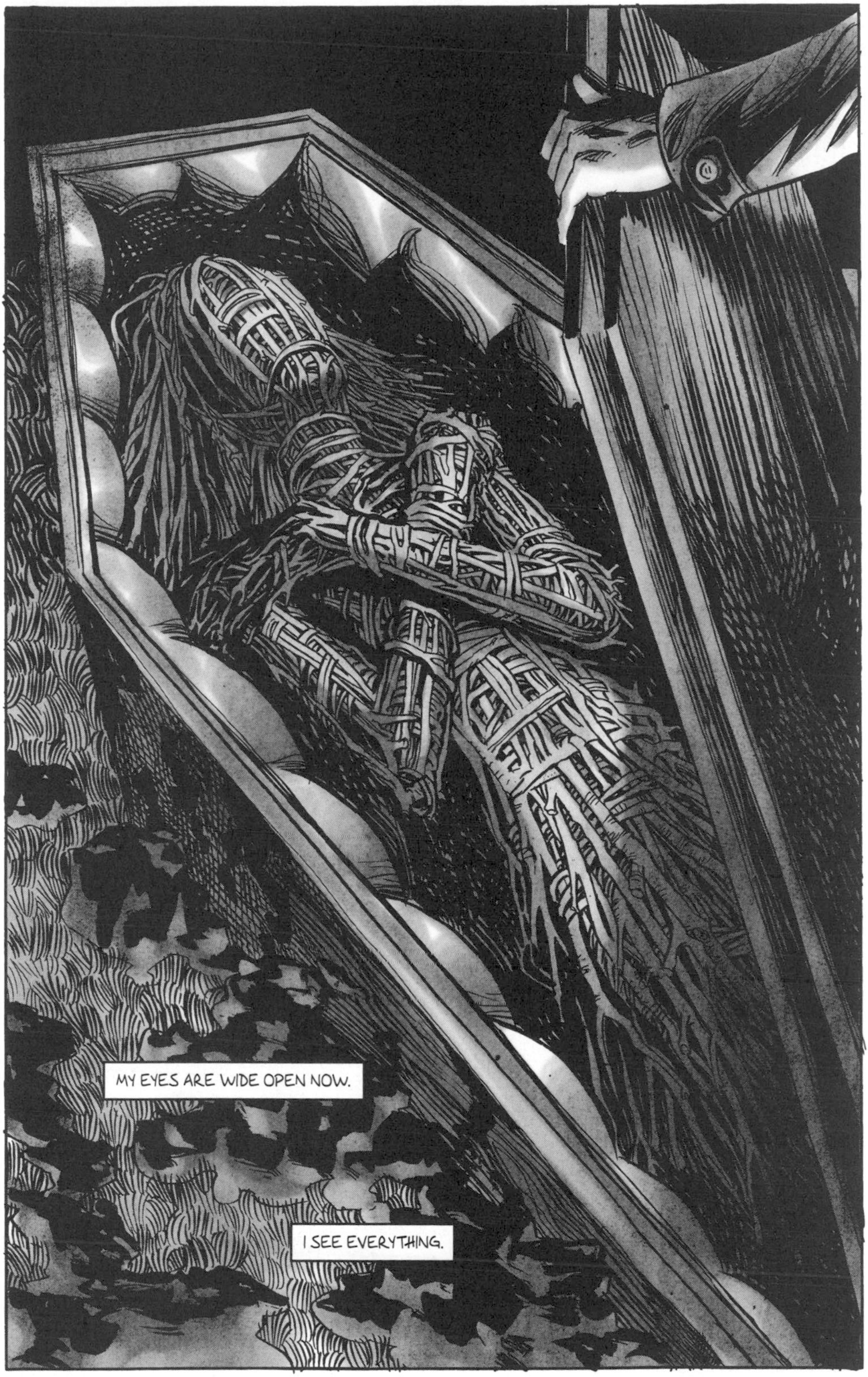
MY EYES ARE WIDE OPEN NOW.
I SEE EVERYTHING.

end of book one

ABOUT THE AUTHOR

Holly Black is the author of contemporary fantasy novels for teens and children. Born in New Jersey, Holly grew up in a decrepit Victorian house piled with books and oddments. She never quite recovered.

Her first book, *Tithe: A Modern Faerie Tale*, was called "dark, edgy, beautifully written and compulsively readable" by *Booklist*, received starred reviews from *Publisher's Weekly* and *Kirkus*, and was included in the American Library Association's Best Books for Young Adults. Holly has since written two other books in the same universe, *Valiant*, a recipient of the Andre Norton Award for Excellence in Young Adult Literature, and *Ironside*.

Holly collaborated with her long-time friend, Caldecott Honor–winning artist Tony DiTerlizzi, to create the best-selling Spiderwick Chronicles. The serial has been called "vintage Victorian fantasy" by the *New York Post*, and *Time Magazine* reported that "the books wallow in their dusty Olde Worlde charm." The Spiderwick Chronicles were adapted into a film in 2008.

She is currently working on a curse magic caper novel called *The White Cat*.

Holly lives in Massachusetts with her husband, Theo, and an ever-expanding collection of books. She spends a lot of her time in cafes, glaring at her laptop and drinking endless cups of coffee.

ABOUT THE ARTIST

Ted Naifeh swooped onto the comics and goth culture scene as the co-creator of *Gloomcookie* with Serena Valentino in 1998. Ted illustrated the first volume of the gothic romance hit before departing to pursue his own projects.

In 2002, he introduced us to the world of Courtney Crumrin, a young loner girl who learns magic from her mysterious and curmudgeonly Uncle Aloysius and uses it to navigate her world of school bullies and bloodthirsty goblins, adolescent peer pressure and deadly coven politics. Courtney's adventures have been published in five volumes: *Courtney Crumrin and the Night Things*, *Courtney Crumrin and the Coven of Mystics*, *Courtney Crumrin in the Twilight Kingdom*, *Courtney Crumrin and the Fire-Thief's Tale*, and *Courtney Crumrin and the Prince of Nowhere*.

Ted's next creation was *Polly and the Pirates*, also published through Oni Press, a swashbuckling tale of proper, rule-abiding young Polly Pringle, who is spirited away from her comfortable boarding school existence by pirates who insist that she is their rightful queen and captain. *Polly and the Pirates* was nominated for a Harvey Award.

Ted has also illustrated six volumes featuring video game character Death Jr. for Image Comics, and is the co-creator of *How Loathsome*, strictly for the 18-and-up crowd.

Ted lives in San Francisco, which influenced his aesthetic from a young age with its magnificently spooky Victorian houses, romantic foggy nights, and significant population of Night Things and other fantastic beings.

ACKNOWLEDGMENTS

A lot of people had a hand in pushing me to try writing a graphic novel and helping me along the way. Thanks to Jon Shestack and Ellen Goldsmith-Vein in particular, for asking me about another faery story and liking the one that I told them. Thanks to Steve Burkow for his calm counsel. I am indebted to my literary agent, Barry Goldblatt, and to my editor, the ever-encouraging and amazing David Levithan. And to Ted Naifeh, who brought these characters to life.

I am grateful to Cecil Castellucci, Kelly Link, Justine Larbalestier, Steve Berman, and Cassandra Clare for pushing me to write better and more cleverly. Thanks to Theo for letting me know when things made sense. And thanks to all of you for putting up with my whingeing.

I was greatly inspired by two books, *The Cooper's Wife Is Missing* by Joan Hoff and Marian Yeates and *The Burning of Bridget Cleary* by Angela Bourke. This book was written with the program Scrivener.

— **Holly Black**

I'd like to thank my girlfriend, Kelly, for pestering Cassie Clare into friendship, and Cassie for suggesting me to Holly. Thanks to both Cassie and Holly for not freaking out at us weird San Francisco kids. I'd also like to thank Phil Falco for the gentle, cheerful nudging, and for being a friendly voice getting me out of bed before the day was completely wasted. Sorry it ran so late.

— **Ted Naifeh**